The Algorithm Plague

A Chilling Probability With Shorter Odds Than You Think…

Dennis J. Hickey

© Copyright 2025 - All rights reserved.

The content contained within this book may not be reproduced, duplicated or transmitted without direct written permission from the author or the publisher.

Under no circumstances will any blame or legal responsibility be held against the publisher, or author, for any damages, reparation, or monetary loss due to the information contained within this book, either directly or indirectly.

Legal Notice:

This book is copyright protected. It is only for personal use. You cannot amend, distribute, sell, use, quote or paraphrase any part, or the content within this book, without the consent of the author or publisher.

Disclaimer Notice:

Please note the information contained within this document is for educational and entertainment purposes only. All effort has been executed to present accurate, up to date, reliable, complete information. No warranties of any kind are declared or implied. Readers acknowledge that the author is not engaged in the rendering of legal, financial, medical or professional advice. The content within this book has been derived from various sources. Please consult a licensed professional before attempting any techniques outlined in this book.

By reading this document, the reader agrees that under no circumstances is the author responsible for any losses, direct or indirect, that are incurred as a result of the use of the information contained within this document, including, but not limited to, errors, omissions, or inaccuracies.

A British Book

Written by a British Author

In British English

Cover Art by : Mister All Sunday

https://99designs.co.uk/profiles/716063

When the Pale Horse of the Apocalypse goes digital....

And I looked, and behold a pale horse: and his name that sat upon him was Death, and Hell followed with him. And power was given unto them over the fourth part of the earth, to kill with the sword, and with hunger, and with death and with the beasts of the earth.

Revelation 6:8

If you enjoy this book in all its eccentric, British, quirkiness, please leave a review on the platform where you bought it. Thank you!

Table of Contents

MIN-JUN—ZERO HOUR 1

THE BANKS 5

DAN—ZERO + 4HRS 9

NATS—ZERO + 8HRS 29

COBRA—ZERO + 10HRS 39

THE TEXEL ADVENTURER—ZERO + 10HRS 53

ROTTERDAM 59

DOROTHY—ZERO + 48HRS 71

DAVID—CAROLINE'S HUSBAND 83

DAVID'S TRIP 89

THE KREMLIN—ZERO + 7 DAYS 115

UNITED NATIONS—ZERO + 1 MONTH 123

ZARA—ZERO + 6 WEEKS 131

PAY DAY—ZERO + 3 MONTHS 147

COBRA POST PAYDAY 153

THE AFTERMATH 159

EPILOGUE 171

Min-jun—Zero Hour

Unique means one. A singleton. You cannot have *very* one or *a bit* one. It is an absolute. So, Min-jun was, without a shadow of a doubt, *unique*. Not because he was a human being, and as such unique, but because of his brain and his interpretation of the world and everything around him. We all see the world in our own way, but degrees of sameness are inevitable. Indeed, more often than not, we behave like sheep, following a common theme. But not Min-jun. He was autistic and a savant, a trope beloved by Hollywood and thriller writers. To them, someone like Min-jun is perhaps the poor man's genius – not a polymath, but fascinating in his own extreme capabilities. That said, they are not a modern myth, and they do very much exist. And Min-jun was an extreme case, as he was the only human being there had ever been with a brain that worked as his did. In fact, the world might never generate another like him, and so it must be said that he was genuinely unique in the history of the human race.

Min-jun's world was mathematics, and not just any mathematics, but a specific branch – software and algorithms. For this branch, Min-jun had a great love. However, love is perhaps the wrong description of his involvement, as it suggests a preference or choice. See, in Min-jun's world, there wasn't really anything else of importance. He was lucky in that his parents were extremely well off, so he had a blessed sort of existence living in a luxurious apartment in Apgujeong-dong in the Gangnam District of Seoul, South Korea. He wanted for nothing and always had access to the newest and best computer equipment that money could buy. Indeed, he spent almost all his waking hours designing his own completely surreal software applications. They meant little to anyone but himself, but to anyone capable of appreciating what he was doing, there was a genuine beauty to behold. His software was precise, efficient, and elegantly simple – and yet simultaneously extremely advanced. He didn't just write the stuff; he read voraciously and was bang up to date on all the very latest ideas in artificial intelligence. He could read the stupidly impenetrable texts generated by the world of academia with ease. He even understood the ludicrous jargon the authors used to try to disguise the fact that most of the time, they weren't even sure themselves what they were talking about. Min-jun just ignored all that and absorbed the concepts they were trying to describe. He would often just adjust what they had been thinking about into a working reality, as he was quite capable of writing very sophisticated AI code if the fancy took him. In fact, had anyone in the field of AI asked, he would have astounded them by demonstrating that he was essentially a full decade ahead of anything they were working on. Yet, no one *did* ask. No one knew anything about Min-jun outside of his close family and his doctor, and it was this that brought the world to its knees.

Whilst it could be said that Min-jun was pretty much a recluse, this, ultimately, was *his* choice. His family looked after him very well and went to great lengths to make sure he was happy and healthy. But this was, of course, before the disaster. And this disaster, as it happened, was caused by an act of kindness. Min-jun's brother had been driving through a suburb of Seoul, enjoying the elevated view from his father's latest Range Rover, when he noticed on the pavement ahead some kids running a garage sale. He spotted an old Texas Instruments PC – one of the very early TI,99/4A units. He stopped on impulse, thinking that Min-jun might like it, and even if he didn't, it might be a bargain. These things were going up in price, after all, so he could always sell it on eBay. And so, he parked the car and went back to haggle. Upon receiving the PC, Min-jun's reaction seemed positive, though it wasn't always easy to be sure. Regardless, after a day or so, Min-jun had dismantled the thing and had it wired up to his own computer. His brother deemed this a success and went on to find a few other legacy machines for Min-jun to mess about with.

Unfortunately, what Min-jun's brother had taken to be enthusiasm on his sibling's part was a sort of shock and horror. Having got the machines, Min-jun was quick to ignore their aesthetics, their hardware, or their history. In particular, what he discovered and came to dislike immediately, was the software that drove them - he hated it. He had never seen BASIC before, nor Pascal, and to him, it was so crude, so clumsy, and so inefficient. Truly, if you had asked him, he would never have described software in these ways – these were concepts that meant little or nothing to him. Min-jun simply didn't see the world in that way. See, the software offended him on a different level, and so he decided to get rid of it. Not by throwing the computers away, mind you, but by destroying the language it was written in. It was nasty and unpleasant and had no use in his eyes, so he figured it should be removed. Of course, this wasn't a rational reaction – at least not in our world - but Min-jun, again, was *unique*, and so his world was also unique (and exceptionally small, to boot). He didn't live on the World Wide Web; he lived at home. For him, it made perfect sense to get rid of all this nonsense. In very little time, he designed a software application that would search out the languages he had come across and didn't like, including FORTRAN, Cobol, Pascal, Basic, CPL, and their ilk, and promptly destroy each and every one.

Had Min-jun understood the scale of the task at hand, perhaps he would have hesitated, but he didn't; his world was his world, and it needed adjusting to make it tidy again. So, he put considerable effort and skill into writing a truly beautiful algorithm that was as advanced a piece of AI as anything that existed. He included several concepts he had been playing around with for some time, the main one of which was self-repetition. The piece of code could repeat itself automatically and exponentially, and of special significance, it could *develop*. Now, this latter element was a mistake, but Min-jun was never to realise this. This was because he had not made the link between the modern software languages he knew and these clumsy old ones. He figured that he simply didn't know all of them, and so he allowed the software to include anything similar to its target. In practice, this meant the algorithm could develop and work its way up through the history of software development at large. He gave the algorithm autonomy. He allowed it to look for anything similar to the programming languages he had chosen to kill. And even though it could be classed as "artificial intelligence," it was, of course, as thick as two short planks. Indeed, it had no sense of judgement or rationality, and what Min-jun had not realised was that these old codes had formed the basis for most modern computer languages – the ones he knew and liked. CPL had morphed into C, C+, and C++. And by making the code free to develop its target, he had, in effect, condemned all software applications to destruction.

You see, Min-jun was nothing if not thorough, and having designed his application and tested it on the computers his brother had gifted him, he set about releasing it into the ether. As was the case, Min-jun had a bank account, so injecting his code into the banking system proved easy. From there, he installed it at the gateway to every search engine he could find. And very soon, anyone looking anything up on the internet anywhere in the world was instantly infected. This wasn't a computer virus in the common sense of the word. Min-jun wasn't trying to steal anything from anyone, for that matter. He wasn't trying to access specific files and extract any data. No, his worm was looking for legacy software to kill – at least, it wanted to do this for a start. Soon enough, though, it would work its way up the development tree. It was no use trying to track it down like some typical virus put out there by the usual well-balanced hacker (with a chip on both shoulders). If your computer could detect this algorithm, it was already too late. Encoding, firewalls, security systems – these are all software of one form or another. And software was the algorithm's conduit, its highway. And on this highway, it would be travelling along at the speed of light.

As an afterthought, Min-jun wrote a short protocol that would turn off his virus if it ever tried to come home and enter his computer. In other words, this unique young man designed a bona fide plague for algorithms and then he went and designed the cure, too. But he would never tell anyone he had done either of these two things, and what's more, no one would ever ask him. For a short while, he would have the only fully functional computer in existence that was switched on, and he, at the very least, would be content.

The Banks

Banks used to be places you put your cash for safekeeping. But the thing is, when you open a bank account, your money isn't yours anymore – you become a *creditor* of the bank. In the past, paper records were kept. Ledgers were based on double-entry bookkeeping, and furthermore, running a bank required people and property. They needed tellers to man the counters to take in and hand out cash. They lent money and charged interest. And they kept large reserves of cash in big vaults. In short, life was simple.

But in the late 1960s and early 1970s, IBM mainframe computers arrived. The ledgers disappeared first, and then the automated tellers arrived, followed swiftly by ATMs or cash machines. And so, all these people the banks employed started to look like expensive liabilities. Computers were advancing at such a phenomenal pace, and so banks began employing them in their trading rooms. And then, of course, came the big breakthrough of the internet. And just like that, all these expensive employees and bank premises could be gotten rid of.

Now, the banks were aided and abetted all the way by politicians of all types, as well as a fair share of philosophies. This was because, in the end, all political careers end in failure, and a nice fat job in a nice fat bank made for a rather lovely soft landing. Margaret Thatcher seemed to worship money. Indeed, she once said that inflation was a sin, and that for her, banks could do no wrong. So, by the turn of the 21st century, cash was becoming the next nuisance.

Cheques had already been attacked, but even venal politicians felt that their abolition was coming too soon. These same people wouldn't let the banks do what they all really wanted to do, which was to charge for the use of cash machines. The fact that this would have amounted to the first form of private tax on income hadn't occurred to the bankers, or if it had, they ignored it. All that said, allowing it would have led to an outcry, so the politicians, for once, stood their ground. Chip and PIN arrived on the scene, though, and eventually, contactless payment became the norm. And so, gradually, cash was being whittled away.

You see, when Min-jun created his killer software, the world was wide open and utterly defenceless. People had unwittingly accepted that when they opened a bank account, they were in effect asking for access to the bank's software systems, and that money didn't exist in reality. Rather, it only existed as an algorithm in a bank's database. Banks still had cash, sure, but at best, this represented about one-tenth of the value of the bank. And on top of that, it nowhere near covered all the cash deposited in the bank at any given time.

So, when Min-jun's virus hit and wiped out all the banks' software, it vaporized pretty much all the wealth at the same time. Anything that wasn't cash or came in the form of paper ceased to exist. Bank accounts no longer existed either, or, at least, not in a form that was of any use to anyone. Rather, they existed in backup systems, which were essentially useless without any software to access them. Cash machines were the first to fail, followed very quickly by all the websites. In the end, people had nothing other than the cash in their pockets.

Of course, people still had assets of one form or another, but an asset is only worth something if you can *sell it*. And in a world with no money, all you can do is exchange it for another asset. Now, Min-jun had not picked on banks as a starting point because he hated them or anything. For him, it was just out of convenience. Nonetheless, it was an inspired choice. Even though they had become ever more automated and dependent on software, the people who ran the banks were never technicians. The banks have always been too big for that. If you want to get to the top in an organisation as big as an international bank, you need to be a corporate politician. You need engineers who can do the technical stuff, and you may even need to use a few contractors. That way, you don't have to pay their pension contributions and sick benefits, let alone give them holidays. These technical types can be a nuisance, really – constantly demanding money to maintain, improve, and protect all this software. So, you end up keeping them in the basement where they belong and do your best to ignore them. This type of attitude means one thing: that of all the organisations riddled with "legacy" software, the banks were up there at the top of the pile – along with the armed forces and government departments – as the easiest prey for Min-jun's plague. Not only did it have plenty to attack right from the start, but it had plenty of opportunities to develop and find similar software languages that were historically linked to the core targets. Regardless, simply wiping out all the legacy stuff to start with caused sufficient havoc, and it all happened – again – at the *speed of light*.

It didn't even take a full 24 hours to spread right across the world. North, south, east, and west – the plague was almost instantly passing from one system to the next and growing exponentially. It used encryption software as a bridge, and passwords were useless from the get-go, they were just another piece of software to be checked out and destroyed if the software language used to form them was too old. Right across the entire globe, the guys in the basements woke up to their worst nightmare. And not one of them had a clue what to do about it.

Dan—Zero + 4hrs

Dan Weston was almost too perfect to be true. He was a 35-year-old Ivy League American. Six foot two, he was a bit small for a basketball player, but he played the game to quite a high level nevertheless. On top of that, he was a lean, fit, good looking blond guy with perfect teeth. He had a degree in corporate law from Yale University, and his parents were wealthy. He'd been married for over 10 years. He had a strict Presbyterian upbringing, he believed in God and America, and he loved his wife and children – and his SIG Sauer 9mm automatic. He was the assistant director of operations for a huge American bank that had a big presence in Asia and a large branch in Seoul.

Dan's big problem in life was that he was a genuinely really nice guy. And he literally did love his gun because, like a lot of Americans, he was addicted to owning one. That said, he was unlikely to ever shoot anyone, and he wasn't really cut out to fight his way up the "Greasy Pole" to become a real highflyer in international banking. That said, his parents were well connected, and he was very good at golf – the other big love of his life apart from his family and firearm. And now, by some strange alchemy, he found himself living in a very nice house in a gated community on the outskirts of Seoul with his wife and two young children.

As an assistant director of operations, Dan essentially looked after a whole heap of contracts for all the technical stuff needed to keep the bank working. What he knew about software and two pence wouldn't pay for his bus fare home, but he did know a good deal about contracts and contract law, and so he spent a modest amount of time at the bank, reading piles of turgid documents very carefully. The rest of the time, he was either on the golf course or socialising with the big expat American community in Seoul. His job wasn't taxing, the pay was excellent, and the golf was great – at least in the summer. All in all, the social life was good, and his kids even went to the American International School, which was pretty good, too, and generally better than a lot of options back home.

So, it came as a bit of a shock when the landline rang at 1:00 am and woke him up. It was the night shift operator at the bank, an Indian guy called Ranjit Singh. Dan had met him once; he was a big guy as tall as Dan with piercing dark eyes and a magnificent beard and turban. At first, Dan had been a bit intimidated by the man's presence, but he soon found him to be very friendly, not to mention highly intelligent and capable. Ranjit apologised for the late-night call, but explained he was simply following the emergency crash procedure, which meant he had to contact Mr. Weston as the operations AD. There was a serious problem at the bank, and Mr. Weston needed to come in urgently.

"Well, I don't know what you expect me to do, Ranjit," said Dan groggily over the phone. "I can't help you out with a software problem. Can't you guys fix it?"

"I'm afraid not, Mr. Weston," responded Ranjit. "That is why I am calling you. The bank won't be able to open later today, and there is a procedure that must be followed."

Dan was speechless for a moment. He tried to pull himself together and wake up; he had only been in Korea in this new job a few months, and so far, life for him had been a smooth road. True, he had worked hard initially to make sure he was up to speed. Furthermore, he had developed a strong sense of duty and liked to do a good job, and so he looked through all the contracts he was responsible for and made sure he understood them well. He even knew that as an operations director, he had overall responsibility for the day-to-day "mechanics" of the bank. But so far, that had only really meant making sure the contractors did what they were supposed to do according to their contracts. He had no actual "shop floor" role at all, and as such, being asked to go in during the wee small hours because the building might not open in the morning was completely outside his comfort zone. But he knew Ranjit was a sensible guy and wouldn't ask if it wasn't absolutely necessary.

"Are you there, Mr. Weston?" Ranjit asked.

"Yes, yes," muttered Dan. "I was fast asleep when you rang. I will get there as soon as I can, give me about 45 minutes."

He put the phone down and explained the situation to his wife, Amy, who had also been woken up by the call.

"It's 1 am," she said, shocked. "What sort of a problem could it *be*?"

Dan scratched his head and stared into space. "I have no idea, but Ranjit on the night shift says the bank might not be able to open in the morning. And his emergency procedure says he must ring me. No exceptions."

Amy looked at him for a moment before saying, "Okay, you grab a shower. I will go and make you a coffee to take with you." He gave her a big hug and headed for the shower. She put on her dressing gown and headed downstairs.

Dan might have had a sheltered life, but he was not a complete idiot. So, by the time he came out of the shower, he knew he was about to face a major problem. He knew that a bank not opening – especially a bank as big as theirs – would be a major crisis of some sort with lots of unknown consequences. And so, he collected his insulated coffee cup, scooped up his keys, and on the way to the car, suggested to Amy that it might be a good idea to stay close to home today and keep the kids off school.

"Do you think it's *that* serious?" she asked, looking alarmed.

"I don't know," replied Dan. "But if they can't open the bank, who knows what will happen? If you're here, I can keep you informed, and I will get back as soon as I can. But I have no idea how long this will take."

"Okay," she said, trying to remain calm. "Keep me in the loop as much as you can, and if you aren't back for breakfast, I will keep the kids at home; they won't mind." She gave him a kiss and watched him drive off, wondering if it was worth going back to bed or not.

As he drove to the bank, Dan passed several others on the way and was surprised to see a few people waiting outside the front doors as he pulled up. He wondered if these must be the start of queues, but he pushed the thought away. He was letting his imagination run away with itself, and anyway, how could these people know there was a problem? Besides, as far as he knew, it was only their bank that had such a problem.

By the time he got to Ranjit's office, everything was eerily quiet. Dan had assumed all the IT guys would be working flat out, but all he found was Ranjit and another Indian guy whom Ranjit introduced to him as Puneet. Dan knew him by sight and seemed to remember he was some sort of software geek. Unlike Ranjit, Puneet was a small, slight guy of a somewhat indeterminate age. Both wore long, sleeved white shirts buttoned at the cuffs, as well as black trousers and black shoes, like a sort of uniform.

After introductions, Dan sat down in the spare office chair. Ranjit's office was small and a little overcrowded with books, computers, and filing cabinets. On what little space Ranjit had on his desk was a blue loose-leaf binder open at a page with what looked like a list of names and telephone numbers.

"Okay, Ranjit, what's going down?" asked Dan.

Ranjit looked at Puneet, who shrugged, put his head down for a moment, and then raised it to look Dan straight in the eye. "The bank is dead, Mr. Weston, Sir. All of our operating software has been irreparably destroyed."

After a moment's silence, Dan gulped and said in as calm a voice as he could manage, "I'm sorry, Puneet. Please just run that past me again, would you?"

"We have been invaded by some new type of virus or worm or whatever you want to call it," said Puneet in a flat and rather tired monotone. "It started with our legacy software."

Dan put his hand up just to pause what Puneet was saying for a moment and asked, "*Legacy* software?"

"Yes, Mr. Weston, Sir. Old stuff that has been around since the days of the old IBM mainframes."

Ranjit interrupted at this point, saying, "It has been a problem for years because no one uses the old software codes any longer. So, if anything goes wrong, you need to try and find an old programmer and dig them out of retirement. They are few and far between, and they know it, so they charge a fortune. Puneet has studied some of the old languages and can sometimes resolve issues for us."

"But no one could help on *this* occasion," Puneet retorted. "Whatever it is that is in the system has not just interfered with the applications. It has completely *obliterated* them. You cannot repair something if it doesn't exist."

Another silence followed.

"Are we so totally dependent on this legacy stuff?" asked Dan.

"A good question, Mr. Weston, Sir," said Ranjit. "And the answer is no. It *is* a nuisance, but we can usually find at least some temporary ways around it. But unfortunately, it didn't stop there."

Ranjit looked at Puneet, who hesitated before carrying on where he had left off.

"It started with the legacy stuff, Mr. Weston, Sir. But it progressed. Whatever it is, it seems to be following the history of software language development and destroying as it goes, at least, that is *my* conclusion. It will take many hours of work to prove if I am right or not, but it is certainly academic, and the damage it has done so far is catastrophic. We had to do something to protect the main database, and so we are going to have to shut everything down."

"Can you *do* that?" asked Dan. "I mean, do you have the authority to do that?"

Ranjit and Puneet looked at each other for a moment. Ranjit was the senior of the two, and so he said, "We had no choice, Mr. Weston, Sir. The bank cannot open anyway because all the operating systems that allow access to the accounts database have been compromised. None of it works, and so we cannot fix it because the applications have not been interfered with. In short, they have been destroyed. If we try to reload the systems, the new applications will also be destroyed. You cannot open the bank until we know what this thing is and how to get rid of it." He paused for a moment, circling the small room. "If it is of any comfort, our friends on the other banks in the city tell us they have the same problem. No bank will open tomorrow, and the ATMs are already defunct."

The horror was slowly beginning to sink into Dan's psyche. "No banks *at all?*" he said almost to himself.

"No," said Ranjit. "So, we believe we have to put in place this emergency procedure. The only copy we have is this hard copy." He lifted up a simple little black box. "Rather stupidly, the procedure has recently been placed on the bank's computer system, which is, of course, inaccessible. And so, we are trying to use the old hard copy, which is out of date and hasn't been maintained. The names and telephone numbers on the list of people to call seem out of date."

Ranjit passed the hard copy to Dan, who rubbed his tired eyes in preparation. He didn't recognise most of the names on the list. So, he did what he thought was the only sensible thing to do: he called his boss, the bank's operations director. But just before he did, he had a flash of inspiration, a moment of hope. And he stopped and looked over at the two IT guys.

"This is a hoax, right?" he said, a small smile creeping across his face. "I am being set up here, aren't I? A little gag on the new guy?"

Ranjit gave him a mournful look for a few seconds and then stood up. "Come with me for a moment, Mr. Weston," he said and walked out of the office.

Dan's moment of euphoria lingered as he thought, "Got you," and fully expected to find everyone hiding around the corner. But it didn't last long. Ranjit walked him through a totally silent IT section – no one sat at any screens, none of the banks of servers buzzing away with flashing LEDs. It was all truly dead. And then he remembered the people queuing up outside. Ranjit stopped and gestured at the dark office; he didn't need to say anything. This was no gag. The two returned to Dan's office, Dan himself crestfallen.

"So, where is everybody then?" Dan asked.

"They have gone home to their families, Mr. Weston, Sir," Ranjit replied simply.

"And you let them go?" asked Dan.

"I could hardly stop them myself, could I, Mr. Weston, Sir? They could see how bad things were and knew that they had no job to come back to tomorrow. They are worried about their nearest and dearest and how they will survive without money. It's different for Puneet and me. Our families are back in India, and our problem will be how to get home if we cannot buy an airline ticket."

Dan looked at him quizzically for a moment. "You guys are already worrying about not being able to get back to India?"

Ranjit's head and shoulders dropped for a moment, and then he looked Dan in the eyes. "Believe me, Mr. Weston, Sir. We can hardly believe the depth and extent of all this ourselves. But there is quite a large community. A network, if you like, of us Asian guys working out here in the banks and finance sector. India generates more software guys than any other country in the world these days, mostly out of Bangalore, and we have been talking to quite a few of them. Puneet and I are well respected in our profession, and we know the guys out there who are at the top of their game. All of us, and I do mean all of us, are shocked and helpless. No one has ever seen anything like this. It's the software equivalent of the atomic bomb going off. So yes, we are worried about getting home."

"Okay," said Dan quietly, after a pause. "Start from the beginning and take me through it again, please. I really need to understand this."

Ranjit thought for a minute and then gave him the best explanation he could think of. Dan learnt that Ranjit was a systems architect. In essence, he looked after the arrangement of the banks of servers that ran the system. Puneet, meanwhile, looked after software maintenance, as it seemed he was something of a software genius. They had taken these positions and worked the night shift because the pay was good, and they sent most of it home to their families. Most of the time, it was pretty boring, so Puneet originally had kept his hands busy by writing software for app developers as a sideline, but when they saw what the legacy guys were earning, he started studying legacy software languages and gradually became something of an expert on the company's old systems. They hadn't quite worked out how to cash in on this yet, but it meant that when the servers started to fail, Puneet was able to spot a pattern.

Dan found that they had even more software monitoring the software. And as such, the system had some capacity to predict problems normally, and it was even capable of working out alternative routes so that Ranjit could set up temporary fixes. So, all in all, this system could illustrate just how the collapse happened. When the first server went down, Puneet had plugged in a diagnostic laptop to see if he could figure out what had gone wrong. He was stunned to come across a nearly blank screen where, instead of the application, he was met with only a few scraps of code.

"It was gone, Mr. Weston, Sir," Puneet stated with a groan. "I couldn't believe what I was seeing at first on that screen. So, I tried to make sense of it for a while, and then my laptop died, as it had been infected. It's like some kind of Algorithm Plague, really."

Quite reasonably, Dan had trouble getting his head around the immensity of the disaster unfolding before him. Had he been less open and honest, and had he been a more typical greasy pole specialist with one eye permanently fixed on what was best for his career development, he might have taken a great deal more persuasion before doing what he did next. But he tended to trust people, and he trusted Ranjit.

So, Dan proceeded to spend the most miserable hour of his life being sworn at and cursed by a collection of truly foul mouthed and unpleasant senior managers as he called them up for an emergency board meeting. They all seemed to assume he was a total moron with his claims of the bank not being capable of opening in the morning, all because of some goddamn computer glitch. Most of them simply told him to "F**k off." Eventually, though, he managed to convince one of them that things really were as serious as they appeared, when he suggested they reach out to other local banks. They did so, and Dan's story was verified. Soon enough, every senior manager understood something truly bad had happened.

Dan was given orders to call in a bunch of secretaries, have his pet geeks on standby, and get the boardroom ready. He opted to make a big pot of coffee in preparation for the meeting. As it dripped, he found himself enveloped in a wave of homesickness. So, he decided to give his father a call, back home in America. It was early afternoon on the west coast, so his dad was pretty chipper and pleased to hear from him at first. But as Dan began detailing what was happening and the foul hour he had just endured with the senior managers, the mood shifted.

His dad went quiet for a moment, and then said, "If what you are saying is true, son, then this won't just be a problem in Korea for long. Let me call you back. I'd better get down to the bank and draw out as much cash as I can and then check with my contacts to see if there's any sign of this so-called plague on this side of the ocean."

Right as he hung up, the first of the bad-tempered board members started to arrive. Dan gritted his teeth in anticipation of further mockery. Nonetheless, he put on a brave face, brought the pot of coffee and a tray of mugs into the boardroom, and began welcoming everyone.

Not every manager turned up; it was far too early in the morning. However, Dan was taken aback to see that among the first arrivals was the chairman of the whole bank. Well into his 60s, though he didn't look it, the chairman was a medium sort of a person – medium height and weight, and not someone who would stand out in a crowd, especially in South Korea. Like Dan, he was also originally from the US. He was a Harvard graduate, and Dan had heard he was even a Navy jet pilot for a while. Nonetheless, he fell in love with a South Korean girl and even had a son here. His days in America were far behind him, and his role as chairman suited his needs – he had no need to ever go back.

Soon after the chairman, the CEO entered the boardroom, looking – as he always did – as though he was off to a fancy dress party, in a suit reminiscent of the *Wolf of Wall Street*. Dan, like most of the other employees in the bank, hated this man's guts. The CEO, another American expat, was well known to be an obnoxious, racist, misogynist, and he was only interested in one thing: *himself*. If he had had a single ounce of grace or a pinch of empathy for the people around him and perhaps had been able to occasionally show a little kindness, he would still be back in America. For, unlike the chairman, the CEO longed to be back in his homeland. But alas, he had none of these saving graces, and he was stuck in Korea. What he *did* have was a huge amount of animal cunning, and as a result, he knew far too much for the chairman to sack him outright. Instead, he had been promoted as far away as possible.

Short, stocky, and always pugilistic, Dan could see that the CEO was equally surprised to see the chairman as he had been himself. It seemed, however, that the chairman and his wife were staying in a hotel nearby, so that he could go and meet his son and daughter-in-law, who were coming back from their honeymoon in Hawaii that morning. Dan sensed that the chairman's presence might protect them somewhat from the nastier extremes of the CEO's behaviour.

Just then, the director of human resources — who doubled as Dan's boss, the operations manager — turned up, treating herself to a cup of coffee and taking a seat. With her arrival, despite the low number of occupants in the room, the CEO cleared his throat, looking like he was keen on getting things moving. And even with the chairman present, the CEO immediately began voicing some unpleasant and aggressive thoughts aimed at Ranjit and Puneet, behaving as though this problem that had brought them here today was entirely their fault. Dan did his best to protect the two, trying to describe the situation for them, but it was hard going. The operations manager, though not as high in the bank's hierarchy as the chairman or the CEO, also did her part in trying to summarise what Dan was saying.

"Okay, Dan, so let me get this straight," the CEO began, after the explanations had ceased. "Peanut and Ramjet here are our night shift guys, and we have been hit by some f***ing huge malware attack. As such, they have had to shut the entire bank down *temporarily*. Is that about right?"

Dan dropped his head for a minute and looked at his hands. "No," he said, sighing. "It is much, much worse than that." When he looked up, he was confronted by an array of annoyed and angry faces. "Whatever it is that has hit us has already wiped out almost all the bank's software. All we have is what Ranjit and Puneet managed to protect. But we can't access that anyway, because they saved it by turning everything off. So, until we know what this is, we cannot risk turning anything back on again."

"Well, what the hell are they doing up here?" asked the chairman. "Shouldn't they be downstairs trying to find out what this thing *is*?"

"We are not equipped to do such a task, Mr. Chairman, Sir," replied Ranjit, who so far had stood his ground with a remarkably steady dignity. "It will require specialist equipment that we do not have here."

"So, where do we find a fix, and how long is it going to take?" the chairman demanded.

Ranjit looked at Puneet, and they chatted together in what Dan had discovered was Gujarati. Apart from a few words of Klingon, Dan wasn't especially knowledgeable of foreign languages, but he was a bit worried the CEO would explode if his two new friends kept this side conversation going on too long. Fortunately, it wrapped up quickly enough, but then Ranjit made the mistake of trying to answer the question honestly.

"We don't really know for sure, Mr. Chairman, Sir," he admitted. "But we think at least two years. Maybe three."

This was met for a second or two by stunned silence before another barrage of foul epithets, courtesy of the CEO. Dan finally managed to intervene in the vitriol, allowing Ranjit to explain what he was talking about.

"Sirs, this is not a hack or a malware attack. It is something *new*. And it is not invading our systems to try and steal data or siphon money or blackmail us. It simply destroys our software," Ranjit explained, mopping his forehead with some paper serviettes. "Normally, if software is wiped for some reason, we would download a fresh copy from head office and reinstall it, but we cannot do that for two reasons. Firstly, we would have to use the internet to download the software, and the internet is the source of the plague, and secondly, we do not know if the servers we have are contaminated or not."

"What do you mean, 'contaminated,' exactly?" asked the chairman.

"Well, often, if you shut down a computer without saving your work, it is lost," responded Ranjit. "So, it may be that switching off a server kills the plague software, but it may not; it may survive in a nonvolatile memory somewhere in the server's circuits and attack the new software when you boot it up again. If this is the case, we would have to replace all the hardware first, and every bank in the world may be in the same position. Therefore, it could indeed be years before we can replace all our hardware."

"So you say," mused the CEO. "But you don't know for sure, right? If we can't download the software we need, let's get it flown in. And whilst we wait, you can test out this contamination idea." He looked pleased with himself for thinking up this little gem.

Ranjit and Puneet looked at each other anxiously, and Ranjit cleared his throat. "That is a very fine suggestion, Sir," he began. "And it might work if we could get some software flown in. But our understanding is that they are trying to get all the planes on the ground as soon as possible. See, it's not just the software at banks that is under threat, but any software connected to the internet."

With that, the chairman went a little pale. Saying nothing, he got up out of his chair and walked out of the boardroom.

Silence reigned briefly until he returned.

"I am sorry for that interruption," he said, sitting back down. "My son and his wife are flying back from Hawaii today, and I just wanted to check that everything was okay."

This changed the mood considerably, and whilst they tried to break down what Ranjit was saying, the truth was that none of them really had a clue as to what he was talking about. And in the end, they told him he better get back to work and damn well find a way to fix this.

Out of any other ideas, Dan took Ranjit and Puneet out of the room and apologised to them as they wandered the halls back toward his office.

"It's okay, Mr. Weston. I'm used to working for arseholes," Ranjit said. "May I suggest something to you?"

"Please do," said Dan. "Anything would help right about now, as far as I'm concerned."

"Someone needs to get in touch with the military."

"What?" said Dan, a bit shocked. "*Seriously*?"

"Yes. Puneet and I have talked about this. This isn't malware, Sir. No one is trying to steal anything. It just destroys software, but *indiscriminately*. So, unless there is a country that is immune—"

For Dan, the penny dropped then. "You mean we could be under attack from Russia or China?"

"Or North Korea," said Ranjit. "But only if their systems are safe. Otherwise, it makes no sense."

"Okay," said Dan, as they reached the office. "Can you two hang around here for a while? I'll come back soon, and then we can figure out some kind of plan here."

Dan headed back to the boardroom. Upon entering, he tried to get everyone up to speed. Still struggling to absorb what was happening, more anger erupted among the senior managers. When Dan suggested they get in touch with other banks again, he was met with a heavy dose of vitriol from the CEO. Even the others shook their heads at this idea. Apparently, no one wanted anyone else to know what a mess they were in, and no one was prepared to break ranks.

Fortunately, one of the other banks was populated by less panic-stricken individuals or, at least, less aggressive idiots at the top. And as it happened, just when Dan felt out of ideas, someone from this bank phoned the chairman on his mobile. And with that call, the occupants of the boardroom could finally face the fact that they were not alone – every bank in the city was in the same position as them. There were even rumours that it was spreading beyond South Korea's borders, too.

Dan wondered if his dad had retrieved his cash in time. At this point, he decided to throw Ranjit's ideas about a foreign attack into the pot - something he promptly regretted, as it set off another shit storm of idiocy from the low-grade psychopath known as the CEO. In his innocence, however, Dan did not realise what he had just done: By bringing up this theory, he was throwing a lifeline to this panic-stricken loser who could see the career he had so deviously fought for so long about to be flushed down the can. And as always, the belief that *if you could blame it on someone else, you might survive* held true. So, a conspiracy theory of sufficient magnitude and credibility was just what he needed. Almost instantly, the CEO stopped hating Dan and seemingly replaced this hatred with silence, which was honestly a relief. Meanwhile, the woman who doubled as the human resources director and operations manager had been sitting stony faced through all of this without a word. She had thought – quite correctly – that foul language was unprofessional and offensive, and so she was affronted by the CEO's display of invective. Only now did she stand up, have a quiet word with the chairman, and then promptly leave the room.

"Now just where is *she* going?" the CEO asked, confused.

"*She* is going to do something useful and get her team to tell the bank staff to stay away today," replied the chairman. "There is no point in them coming in until we have a better picture of how bad this truly is."

The CEO mulled this over for a short while to see if it affected him in any way. Deciding it didn't, he grunted his assent.

Dan had still found himself wondering about the people outside the building – as well as about his wife and children at home. In fact, he surprised himself by suddenly deciding that he was wasting his time in this office. So, he excused himself, giving the impression he was just off to the bathroom. As he left the room, though, he caught a glimpse of the expression on the CEO's face – it was a look of fear, surprisingly. *Naked fear.*

Walking out into the hallway once more, he remembered a speech an old friend of his father's had given him before he started work. The man had sat Dan down and said, "Look, I don't want to destroy your enthusiasm for this new adventure in your life but do be careful. You may think you are about to leave college and enter a great meritocracy, where you'll be rewarded for hard work and a good performance. But sadly, what you're really entering is the corporate world. It's much more like a *creep*ocracy. You'll find it difficult at first to understand why the people you work for are in the jobs they're in, and eventually, you'll see that it isn't *what* you know that counts as much as *who* you know. Or better yet, who you *suck up to*. Bottom line, the corporate definition of a 'team player' is someone who keeps his trap shut and does what he's told. So, if you're intelligent, innovative, and articulate, you'll probably be labelled a smart-arse. And so, Dan, my advice to you is to play the game but keep your self-respect. This will slow down your rate of promotion, but you know what? You'll remain a human being and get to work with people who you'll eventually get to call *friends*."

As the memory faded, Dan realised that all this now applied to the CEO. He wasn't particularly intelligent or able, but he had been very adept at understanding which way the corporate wind was blowing. He had learned the latest jargon. He had tied his wagon to the most likely rising star. He never showed his obnoxious nature to his superiors; he kept that for his minions. But in his case, he had not been 100% percent successful in this, and his sheer nastiness had leaked out. Rather than sack him, they had banished him to Korea. And so, here he was. All alone with his third wife divorcing him back in the US. All that conniving and twisting and turning to slide his way up the greasy pole, and he was stuck in Korea in a company rental house without a friend in the world.

Dan headed down in the lift, thinking of how Ranjit and Puneet must still be sitting in his office in deep thought. He couldn't help but grin to himself, even though he knew it was uncharitable of him to leave them like that. He couldn't risk popping into his office at this point, so he phoned his office phone on his cell. When a confused Puneet picked up, he thanked the two of them for waiting, but said they had better get home as there was nothing to do and no point trying to explain anything else to that boardroom of frustrated managers. They exchanged addresses and telephone numbers, and then Dan promised Ranjit he would try and get through to the military headquarters as soon as he could.

Wandering through the front lobby, Dan managed to track down the security guard, whom he asked to take a look at the CCTV cameras behind his desk. One of the monitors displayed the queue outside – it was getting longer. Dan phoned the head of security and tried his best to give him a clear and concise description of the situation. He advised the man to either get down to the building or simply clear his staff out, and whilst he was at it, call the MD and tell him to evacuate, too.

The security chief was stunned on the other end of the line. "Why me?" he asked, "Why don't *you* tell them? You're there, I'm not!"

"Because they won't believe me," replied Dan. "And quite frankly, I have had enough of trying to explain to those idiots what's happening. I think it's going to get ugly here later, so I'm getting out whilst I can. You should leave it to the police to protect the building. You guys don't get paid enough. Anyway, I'm getting out of here before they start queuing past the exit ramp of the car park."

Instead of waiting for a response, Dan put the phone down and told the security guard to also get out whilst he still could. And then he was off. It occurred to Dan as he drove away that this was likely the end of his career in banking. And oddly enough, he found he wasn't the slightest bit bothered. He knew that the next few days would likely get deeply dramatic, and so he began brainstorming a reasonably good plan to keep his family safe.

Dan had met Amy back home in the US via the church their families had both attended, and found out the two had had a mutual interest in golf. Her family was not quite as well off as his, but they were far from poor. She had studied art history for a while before they were married and worked in a local museum. She had a sister just 18 months older than her, and they were very close. Part of the reason they came to South Korea was that her sister was married to an army dentist and they had been posted to the USAG Yongsan base in Seoul.

When he phoned Amy, he ended up waking her up a second time. He told her to book them all into the Dragon Hill Lodge Hotel on the military base for a week on the basis that they were relatives of army personnel. He told her that he'd explain everything in detail once he got home. He figured the hotel would take their credit card details for now without actually trying to draw on it, allowing them to work something out later.

Amy was not given to panic. She was a level-headed person, in truth, and so she had done as requested by the time he arrived home, despite her confusion. The two sat down in the kitchen, sharing some coffee and breakfast as he explained the dilemma.

"The bank is dead, Amy," he said. "And I do mean *dead*. Worse yet, it's likely not the only one. As Korea wakes up today, people are going to find out that they can't access their bank accounts anymore. And that includes *us*. The only money we have is what cash we can scrape together."

"So, why book us into a hotel if we can't afford it?" Amy asked quite sensibly.

"It's part of the army base. And I want to talk to Kate and Henry, but I don't want to just dump on them without some explanation." He took a big sip of his coffee and sighed. "I don't know how the next few days are going to work out, truthfully. This is unprecedented, and I want to do the best I can to make sure we are safe. Everyone in the hotel will be in the same position as us, and maybe we can move in with Kate and Henry and the kids once things have started to unfold; they have that big old Winnebago parked in their backyard. Maybe we could camp in there for a while if it gets to that. For now, we need to pack up all our valuables and everything else we can fit into the SUV and get over to Yongsan. I want to talk to Henry as soon as I can. We can go there first. We won't be able to check into the hotel until this afternoon, anyway."

So, about three hours later, as the sun began to finally light up the sky, Dan and Amy gathered up their belongings and bemused children and set off across the city to the Yongsan base. Being a major, Henry was allowed married quarters in the form of a modest detached house. This, then, was where Dan drove, as Amy phoned ahead to explain what was happening, all whilst trying not to feed into any panic. This would be on the news channels soon enough – the panic could wait a few minutes more.

Once they arrived, the families together came to understand that there was some sort of crisis occurring with the banks and the ATMs. However, the news media still hadn't fully grasped the scale of this problem. Dan was able to offer some of the significant details and theories explained earlier to him by Ranjit. Henry thought about this for a few minutes and then opted to call his commanding officer. They had a brief conversation, and Henry was told to stay put and wait for a return call. It came about 20 minutes later, and Henry asked Dan if he wouldn't mind coming with him to explain what he had told them to the camp commander. So, leaving the others behind, the two men set off for the main admin offices, one of the older buildings built by the Japanese.

Approaching the camp commander's office, both were a bit nervous. They had to wait a little while in the outer office before being invited into a large and very business-like office - nothing like the cosy luxury of the bank's offices for senior staff, as Dan noted. Waiting for them were the general and a couple of senior officers. Dan wasn't sure what rank they all were, but Henry did a bit of smart saluting. Dan almost felt as though he should join in for a moment but ultimately figured it would be best not to.

After introductions, they all sat around the conference table in front of the general's desk, and coffee was served. The general thanked Dan for coming in and asked him if he could give everyone his account of what, precisely, was going on. Dan was struck by the calm air of authority these guys exuded. Having recently been witness to a bunch of largely pathetic idiots panicking, it was very reassuring to now be able to talk calmly and sensibly. So, he told the story of Ranjit Singh calling him in, and everything that followed. When he got to the bit about Puneet's theory and legacy software, the general and the other two officers visibly stiffened and gave each other telling looks. One of them asked Dan to go back a bit and go over what he had just said in more detail. Dan noted to them that he wasn't an IT guy – his background was contracts. Regardless, he did his best to explain the legacy software stuff in the way Puneet had explained it to him. He went on about how the virus spread in a way that seemed to be moving along a timeline, matching software application development. When he was done, Dan said again how this wasn't his area of expertise – and that it didn't make much sense to him, even still.

There was a big pause with more looks exchanged. Finally, the general asked Dan if he thought these two guys, Ranjit and Puneet, would be happy to come in and talk to them. Dan figured they probably would. But he made sure to tell the general that the two were most concerned about getting home to India, and that getting there might take precedence for them over this meeting.

The general looked puzzled upon hearing that. "They want to leave the country? Why?"

"Because both Ranjit and Puneet are of the opinion that this isn't fixable," Dan responded. "It's not going to be one of those bank problems that got sorted in a few hours or days, because *they're the guys* who do all the sorting and fixing. And they believe they're helpless."

"I see," said the general quietly.

"They had to close down the bank's entire computing system in order to protect what was left," Dan went on. "And they had no idea how to reboot it safely. So, until someone figures out what's happening and comes up with a cure, they're stuck. As far as I know, they have no access to money and no way of buying an airline ticket."

"Mr. Weston," said the general, looking deep into Dan's eyes. "I need your honest opinion here. Do you think this is a hack gone wrong, or do you think it's a full-scale cyber-attack?"

"I'm not qualified to say, General," Dan responded simply. "But Puneet didn't think it was a hacker. No one is gaining anything from it. This thing: it isn't stealing anything or trying to blackmail anyone like ransomware. It's just systematically destroying software. Puneet called it an 'Algorithm Plague.'" Dan thought for a minute longer, then added, "If it is some sort of government, sponsored cyber-attack, it should be pretty obvious where it's coming from."

"What makes you say that Mr. Weston?" asked the general.

"Because they would be idiots not to protect their own systems. And any country that's not affected by this will stick out like a sore thumb," Dan responded confidently. "Though there is a flaw, I think... in that logic." He paused for a moment. "See, from what I understand of this Algorithm Plague, if I can call it that, it's travelling via the internet, and it's indiscriminate. This essentially means that no bank in the world will be safe. So, if this *is* a cyber-attack by a hostile country, then they will have to protect their banks as well as their systems."

"Well, I cannot deny the logic of what you just said, Mr. Weston," said the general, rising to his feet. "If you are right, time will tell. But I think for now, if you can put us in touch with Ranjit and Puneet, we will talk to them and, in return for their help, see if we can help get them back home."

"They will crawl over broken glass for you if you can do that, General," said Dan, with a sad smile.

The meeting was over, and with a mixture of handshakes and salutes, Dan and Henry headed back towards the car.

"I think you struck a nerve with that legacy software stuff," said Henry as they pulled away from the admin offices. "From what I can see of the army's IT systems, I bet they are full of software that should have been replaced years ago. Which means..."

"This isn't good, is it, Henry?" asked Dan.

"No," said Henry. "Not a bit. Let's get back to the girls and the kids and hunker down in front of CNN for a bit."

NATS—Zero + 8hrs

Jon was the shift engineer for the major NATS (National Air Traffic Services) site at Swanwick in southern England. In his early thirties, a graduate of Manchester University and a keen cyclist, he was perhaps a little overqualified for the rather mundane job of looking after the banks of servers that kept the site running. He should have been earning more money writing software somewhere with more sociable hours, but he was licking his wounds after an unhappy breakup with his fiancée and was happy to retreat into a quieter existence. The night shift suited his need to withdraw.

Though his withdrawal wasn't total he still kept in touch with a circle of friends and acquaintances, many of them in the IT industry he had just received an email from the friend who'd gotten him the job in the first place. His friend worked in a different part of the organization at a separate site and kept normal hours, so Jon was surprised to see a message pop up marked urgent. He was alarmed when he read it.

Jon, something mega is happening. I'm sending this from my mobile my computer is dead. Something really bad is going down. You need to check your systems!!!

Jon was still staring at the message when his own computer screen went blank. The machine was still powered up, but completely unresponsive. He tried various key combinations that the average person wouldn't even know existed nothing. His system seemed wiped clean.

He grabbed his phone and called his friend.

"What the hell is going on, Kev? My computer's just died and I mean died. I can't access any part of it. It looks like it's been wiped clean!"

"I know," said Kev. "Same here. They'll be queuing outside your office any minute now, but it's not just NATS. I'm getting messages from all over. Something's out there on the internet. You need to get the planes with connectivity to switch it off, or they won't have anything to fly with. I've got to go I'll catch you later."

Jon felt slightly sick to his stomach. The office phone rang, snapping him out of his daze. It was the night shift supervisor.

"Hi," said the supervisor, having momentarily forgotten Jon's name. "I seem to have a problem with my computer. It's just gone blank. Can you help at all?"

"I'm sorry," said Jon. "This may sound extreme, but I think you need to declare a critical security alert and ground all aircraft if that's possible?"

To the supervisor's credit he'd been an air traffic controller once and wasn't prone to panic, his response was measured. He didn't assume Jon was stupid or insane. In fact, he now remembered they were lucky to have Jon, given his background at GCHQ.

"Could you give me a little more detail?" he asked.

Jon did his best.

"My computer's down too, and as far as I can tell, it's been wiped. I can't access anything. This doesn't look like hacking, it's destruction. Just before it died, I had an email warning from a colleague that something was going wrong. I spoke to him just now. He's at Head Office in Whiteley. It seems we're under attack from something extremely dangerous via the internet. And if it can kill our computers despite all the firewalls and protections we have, you have to ask: how far can it get into the rest of the system?"

"What exactly are you saying?" asked the supervisor, mainly to buy time. He suspected he already knew.

"If this... thing can sweep in and wipe us out, what about the aircraft system software?"

"But surely," said the supervisor, "if you're flying at 30,000 feet, you wouldn't be connect—" He broke off mid-sentence.

"Oh shit."

"Exactly," said Jon. "In-flight internet connectivity. They're not isolated. And even our own systems must be at risk and we can't just shut them down; that would be a disaster in itself."

"Are you sure it's that serious?"

"Well, you saw your screen die," said Jon. "What if that was a cockpit display? I can't guarantee it won't be that serious and neither can you. We should ground everything until we know what's happening. Get the pilots to disable internet connections. Have cabin crew check whether passengers are having device issues if they are, the plane could be in deep trouble."

At that moment, both Jon and the supervisor had people arriving with more reports of system failures. "OK," said the Supervisor. "I will flag up a maximum critical alert. We can send out what you've just suggested as an instruction, get everything down as soon as possible and stop any further flights. I'll let Prestwick know and see if I can contact our friends in Europe. It's 9/11 all over again."

What followed was far more difficult. There was significant resistance from people who, having worked hard to develop their careers to a point where they finally had a degree of power, suddenly found themselves faced with a decision that could make or break them. Quite a few just wanted to hide in a corner somewhere and let someone else decide. But enough pushed hard enough, and Captain Phil Glover — the very experienced pilot of a large, modern twin-engine, wide-bodied passenger aircraft on its approach to Heathrow after crossing the Atlantic received a strange communication from the NATS air traffic centre behind him.

He turned to his copilot.

"Well, that's a bit weird. Can you get the manual out and see what the protocol is for turning off the internet connection to the plane? We've just been instructed to do it urgently."

Phil pressed the button that summoned a member of the cabin staff. When the young woman arrived, he asked her to walk down the cabin aisle and ask any passengers with laptops or iPads if everything was OK. He explained he wanted to know if any of them were having problems with their devices and to report back as quickly as she could. Just before she left, he added,

"We're about to turn off the internet connection, so I'm not interested in complaints about that. I need to know if anybody's device has packed up. OK? Quick as you can — try first class first; that lot are always tapping away."

She looked a bit bemused but set off. Meanwhile, the copilot had figured out which button turned off the internet.

"Mind telling me what's going on?" he asked, not unreasonably.

"NATS says there's some sort of computer systems crash spreading via the internet. They're worried it will affect our flight control systems. Apparently, if you're infected, everything goes blank — hence the query about the passengers' devices. If they're all OK, we should be."

"But our systems aren't directly linked to the internet, are they?" asked his copilot, Pat Cussens.

"I'm not sure I'm best qualified to answer that, Pat. You'd think not, but we're transmitting data about engine performance via satellite. I don't know if there's any crossover."

There was a knock at the door. The stewardess returned.

"One of the passengers in first class is complaining his laptop has packed up. He seems to think it's our fault."

"OK," said Phil. "Everyone should be in their seats ready for landing. We've got the undercarriage down and the flaps extended. We should be OK. Go back and get all the cabin staff in their seats and strapped in."

As she turned to go, all the screens in front of him went blank — and the engines shut down.

"Oh shit," was Phil's uninspiring but honest response to this momentous event. He looked out at the rapidly approaching runway and tried to remain calm. Panicking wouldn't help.

He was in a modern passenger aircraft with "fly-by-wire" controls, meaning he had no manual control and no time. Normally, everything was backed up with plenty of redundancy to guarantee safety. But that didn't help if everything died at once.

What he did have were good flying instincts. He'd been flying since his dad took him up in a glider as a teenager. This monster wasn't a glider. It had wings and momentum, but it also had two huge engines and a massive undercarriage hanging below. The nose was dropping as aerodynamic drag on the bottom rotated the plane. With no engine thrust to counter it, it would keep doing so.

He could see they would nearly make the runway but not quite. If only he could pull the nose up a fraction. Maybe they could make it. If he could just avoid the front wheel hitting soft ground...

Then, a random memory popped into his overstressed brain. As far as Pat was concerned, Phil went a bit insane. He picked up the cabin mic and screamed:

"Everyone at the front of the plane get up and run to the back! We're about to crash. If you want to live, unbuckle your seatbelts and run to the back! Get to the back now! Pack yourselves in the galley! Throw yourselves over other people in their seats! But do it now! MOVE, MOVE, MOVE!"

To their credit, quite a lot did. Some were too stunned, some too old, fat, infirm, or simply frozen by fear. The two pilots stared at the runway. This wasn't a light aircraft — you couldn't "feel" anything through the seat of your pants. The weight shift would take time to affect such a huge inertial mass.

Were they imagining it, or did the nose lift just a little? They weren't sure. But they hit.

All aircraft landings are controlled crashes. At 180–200 knots (200–230 mph), the real danger is not horizontal speed but the vertical rate of descent. Without engines, the plane was dropping like a brick.

But the front wheels didn't hit first. The main gear hit just on the runway's edge. A few feet less, and they'd have hit soft ground and disintegrated. They hit hard, far too hard, all the tyres burst. Overhead lockers burst open; duty-free bottles became missiles.

The undercarriage held amazingly. But the plane began to slide. Almost 300 tonnes at 200 mph generates massive kinetic energy. With no thrust or brakes, friction was their only hope. But friction can be a bit random. One side dug in more than the other, the plane slewed one way, then back. Finally, the left undercarriage collapsed, the engine hit the runway, and the plane lurched and rotated before sliding to a stop, half on and half off the runway. At each stage, passengers were battered and terrified. But they were alive and no fires started. The cabin crew recovered first, got the doors open, and deployed the chutes. Despite injuries, people scrambled out. Adrenaline helped. The two pilots completed the emergency shutdown (though they doubted it mattered) and helped evacuate.

Standing together afterward, they looked at the debris-strewn runway.

"I don't suppose now's the time to go look where we hit?" said Phil.

Pat didn't answer. He stared at the sky, pale as a sheet. Phil followed his gaze.

"Jesus," he said. "It's an A380."

The giant jet seemed to hang in the air, nose down, silent. It disappeared beyond the M25, then a vast plume of water rose.

"Wraysbury Reservoir," Pat said. "Straight in."

They watched the plume settle. A rainbow formed briefly. Neither man spoke it's hard to talk when you're sobbing.

Other passengers had seen it, one woman had dropped to her knees genuflecting and praying but she collapsed in a heap when a few seconds after the impact they heard the deafening crash, it reached them as a sort of boom. Pat finally found his voice first, though he spoke through his sobs.

"I think in answer to your question, walking down to the end of the runway is perhaps not a good idea, in fact staying here where we are now is looking like a very bad idea." Phil looked at him and nodded but neither of them moved. "By the way" said Pat "I have to know what gave you the mad idea to send all the passengers to the back?"

"Well" said Phil as he dried his eyes on the clean hanky his wife always insisted he should have with him, "I've always been fascinated by the old Sunderland flying boats," he was struggling a bit to talk but he ploughed on "they were always built with a civilian version in mind it was called the Empire, after the war some were converted to civilian use and they built a few new ones called the Sandringham, I watched a documentary about them on the TV once. It was another age, with stewards in red Bolero jackets and white gloves, flying to Cairo meant an overnight stop in the Med and they used to all get together for a party. They interviewed some of the pilots that were still alive and I remember one saying that the passenger cabin had a bar at the back, he used to have to get ready to adjust the trim when he announced it was open as all the passengers got up and shot to the bar to be first in the queue."

"And that just Popped into your head?" asked Pat, he was hugging himself and starting to shiver, "shit" he said, "Is this the shock setting in?"

"Maybe" said Phil, "Perhaps we should go to an Ambulance and get checked out. Do you think it worked?"

"I have no idea," said Pat "If it helps, I am pretty sure the nose did come up a fraction, maybe that is all we needed, maybe that was the difference between us and the poor buggers in the reservoir because it was a bloody close-run thing, I know that much."

Phil stopped suddenly doubled up and was sick on the side of the runway. He was becoming increasingly grateful he had a hanky.

"I don't think I can cope with not knowing." He said, "You go and find an ambulance I'm going to see if one of the ground staff will drive me down to look."

"You're not going without me" said Pat "I can have my nervous breakdown later."

So, they went over to a runway maintenance vehicle parked near the crashed plane, the driver was stood by the open door talking on a radio and they pleaded their case with him. He was a big guy in his late forties wearing a yellow hard hat and a high vis jacket,

"This isn't exactly a safe place to be at the moment you know," was his initial response "and you two should be seeing the medics not having little joy rides down the runway."

"We do realise that" said Phil "But we just had the exact opposite of a joy ride up it and I won't be able to sleep again unless I know how close we were to dying, I need to know if what I did worked." The guy looked at him for a moment, taking in the sight of these two pilots who were clearly shocked out of their wits, he could see one of them shivering and said.

"OK but we need to do this quickly, I need to check out how much debris is on the runway, though to be honest at the moment I don't really know why I'm bothering there isn't much I can do about it." so they got in his car and shot off down to the end of the tarmac. Phil found what he was looking for, the impact point of the main undercarriage, right on the very edge of the runway,

"Bloody hell" said the maintenance guy "That was to close for comfort, wasn't it?" The two pilots just nodded in unison, trying to take in what they were seeing, "It looks to me as if the back tyres on the main undercarriage actually missed the end of the runway, if you had been just a few metres further back when you hit it, or you hadn't been lined up so perfectly you would have ripped the undercarriage straight off." They nodded again,

"I think that answers your question," said Pat. They all got back in the car and the runway maintenance guy took them to one of the ambulances and an uncertain future. He set off back to his control centre and got his boss on the radio.

"I think we should gather all the team together in the underground car park," was his opening gambit.

"What on earth for?" asked his boss,

"Did you see the A380 go down?"

"Yes, it was horrendous."

"OK, well I've just been talking to the pilots of this crash and everything in the cockpit went blank and the engines stopped, 'Fly by Wire' became 'No Wires to Fly By' so they had no control over anything. Think about it, if the engines on that A380 had kept going for another thirty seconds, we would have been toast, forty seconds it would have hit the centre of the airport. We need to try and get somewhere safe, if there was a bomb shelter we should head for it. We can't do anything useful in the next hour and by then what is up there will have landed one way or another, when you are out here it feels like you are in the middle of a dart board."

"Jesus," said his boss "that's an awful lot of tragedy you just described."

"Yes" he replied, "I don't see the point in adding any of us to it."

"Fair enough" said his boss "We don't get paid enough to put our lives on the line, I'll see you in the garage."

COBRA—Zero + 10hrs

Professor John Davenport was beginning to feel his age – and he was only 45. He had been up most of the night talking to his wide network of contacts about the developing nightmare, and he had gone into work the following morning to talk to his team about what was going on – and what they could actually do about it. As head of the computer science department at Imperial College London, he understood more than 99.9998% of the population about the burgeoning crisis, and yet what he knew still didn't amount to a hill of beans.

He and his team had only just begun to understand that whatever it was, it wasn't a "hacker" in the normal sense of the word. And furthermore, they had determined that it seemed to start with legacy software. From there, it moved upwards through the history of software development, which, in itself was almost idiotically bizarre. What *really* worried all of them was the utter ruthlessness of the thing and the way it seemed to be wiping out software algorithms altogether, rather than trying to hijack them or steal from them. John's team at the university had tried to isolate everything from the internet as soon as they could and had, in fact, managed to turn everything off in time.

In the morning meeting, one of John's associates brought him a message from the admin asking him to ring a number urgently. He had been so overwhelmed by all the calls he had received in the last several hours that he had turned his phone off. Recognising the number presented to him, though, he realised it would be time to plug it back in.

John Davenport, as it happened, was a well-connected man. He was a very clever and competent computer systems engineer and designer. He had studied his subject at arguably the best university in the country for this subject – the University of Manchester, but he came from a comfortably middle-class family in London who had good connections in both politics and the media. So, apart from his work at the university, he was also on several committees and an advisor to the Civil Contingencies Secretariat via the Department for Culture, Media and Sport, which always amused him as an engineer. However, the government, in its wisdom, had decided that John's department, in an emergency situation, would be responsible for all things related to the internet. He had confronted this fact before with Whitehall. These people thought technology meant computers and the internet meant the media – simple as that. It worried him sometimes that the people supposedly running the country could be so totally pig-headed when it came to technology. Regardless, he never worried for long about things he couldn't change, and he had come to the conclusion that "running the country" was a wildly inaccurate statement; generally, those tasked with this job had about as much influence as next door's cat.

But this number before him now – John recognised it as the departmental secretary. This was the person who set up the meetings he attended to discuss all things "internet," which mainly involved the government trying to get a grip on it in the first place. So, he was a bit surprised when, after ringing the number, the voice on the other end asked if he was free that afternoon to attend a COBRA meeting at Whitehall. A car would be sent to pick him up.

And so it was: At 2:00 p.m., a sleek black Jaguar rolled up. Soon enough, John found himself on the pavement outside No. 20 Whitehall and feeling a bit nervous.

He was ushered into the Cabinet Office Briefing Room, the title of which formed the acronym "COBRA." There are several of these rooms, but today it was the main one – long, narrow, and filled with a honey-coloured conference table and a set of screens covering the end wall – which would host today's meeting.

The room was already packed with most of the different sections of the Civil Contingencies Secretariat present, and to John's amazement, the head of GCHQ was here, too, along with someone he recognised as a pretty high up member of the Bank of England. This did nothing to settle his feeling of nervousness as he sat next to the super spy from Cheltenham. He knew him by sight and reputation, so he said hello and shook his hand just as the prime minister entered the room, making her way straight to the head of the table. Apparently, she would be chairing this meeting.

Newly elected after a pretty bloody internal battle within her own party, this would be the prime minister's first major crisis. John could not help but feel a bit sorry for her. He was certainly curious to see how she would perform. Sitting back in his chair, he figured his best tactic would be to simply listen and only speak when spoken to. He was soon to find out this strategy wasn't going to work too well.

The PM said good afternoon to everyone, thanked them for coming, and started matters off.

"As you know," she said, "We have a major crisis with the banks. There has been a collapse in their software systems brought on by some sort of worldwide computer virus. There is not a cash machine in the country that is working, and I am told the banks cannot access anyone's accounts, including ours." She gestured to everyone in the room at this point and got a few wry smiles in return.

"What we need to try and establish, then," she continued, "is how soon we can recover this situation and what, if anything, we have to do in the interim to protect the public. I understand that this crisis may not be limited to the banks, but I would like to discuss this issue first, and then we can go around the table to find out how the rest of you are coping. And so, with this in mind, I would like to ask Professor Davenport from Imperial College London to try and give us his best description of what the problem is and how long it will take to fix. Would that be alright, Professor?"

Everyone turned to look directly at John. He really wasn't expecting this, but he swallowed hard, tried to get his thoughts in order, and cleared his throat.

"I will do my best, Prime Minister," he began, "but you have to realise what we are trying to deal with here is new. That is, it isn't just a hacker or a set of criminals... and unless you find a country that is entirely immune from its effects, I would suggest it is not state-sponsored."

"Then what on earth is it?" asked the PM, flatly.

"I don't know, but it kills algorithms," replied John. "It doesn't invade your system to steal data or money or secrets. It just kills the software. And so, the banking system is, well, *dead*."

"We understand that, Professor," said the PM, "but what we want to try and figure out is how long it will take to get it back up and running. Could you enlighten us?"

"Well... It might be *years*, Prime Minister," said John, almost cringing as he said it.

"'Years'? Did you really just say '*years*'?" the PM exclaimed, incredulously. "Surely not, that's ridiculous."

"All I know is that until we track this thing down – capture it, essentially – and then figure out how to kill it, no one can connect their computer to the internet. And if they have already been invaded, then as long as their computer is switched on, it will be systematically destroying the software on it. As far as the banks are concerned, this has already happened, hundreds of millions of lines of software. In fact, billions have been destroyed already. Everyone's bank account details may still be stored on backup hard drives within the banks, but there is no way of accessing them."

John paused for breath and looked around the room. He clearly had the full attention of his audience, so he decided to plough on.

"So, basically, we can't turn anything back on until we have trapped this thing and learned to kill it. And when we do, we have a massive job on our hands trying to reboot the banking system, which, quite frankly, was a hell of a mess before this even happened. It isn't for me to say what the public will do if they ever get access to their cash again, but it seems obvious that if we just put things back as they were, the first thing anyone with any sense is going to do is draw out all their cash. So, yes, Prime Minister, I think the answer to your question is *years*. If we are extremely lucky, perhaps it will be just a matter of months before we have figured out what this thing is and how to kill it. And after that, you are looking at scorched earth in terms of the banks; they've been rushing headlong into computerised banking for years now to save money. So, honestly, I think we all know what the banks really want to do, and that's get rid of cash altogether. Ultimately, then, this hasn't just destroyed all of that ambition. It's completely wrecked all their systems."

The room was still silent. John had expected it to suddenly erupt with dissenting voices once he was done speaking, but, of course, the room was full of civil servants in a crisis, and he had already broken every rule in the book by sticking his head above the parapet and expressing an opinion. Even worse, he had criticised the banking system; these were all middle to high-ranking civil servants who all knew that climbing the greasy pole of promotion involved saying nothing unless you were asked a specific question.

But after several heavy moments, the representative from the department of health said in a quiet and calm manner, "Oh dear." All eyes shifted to her. "Then the news I am getting will be equally terminal, I suppose?"

John looked at her, then to the silent PM, then back again.

Sighing, he said, "I am afraid so. If your computer systems have been linked to the internet over the last 24 hours, then they are infected, and all you can do to limit the infection is to turn them off. If you don't, then they will be destroyed, and when we reach a point where you can turn them back on again, they will need significant repairs. Their usefulness will be compromised, too. See, the internet is already dead, and as it was used to transmit itself initially, this bug has killed all the servers running the net. That means there's no more email, and unless you have your email archive stored on a safe hard drive, all your emails will have been lost along with any unsecured data of any sort."

A very smartly dressed gentleman on the other side of the table, who turned out to be a two-star general, said, "Presumably, if your systems are fully encrypted, this won't apply?"

John was about to respond when the head of GCHQ, seated right next to the general, cut in: "I'm sorry to say, General, that encryption is no barrier. Your systems in the defence sector are as wide open as everyone else's. If I were you, I would get all our ships and aircraft home as soon as you can. And I do mean *all* of them. I don't want to jump the queue, Prime Minister, but I can support what the professor is saying. You see, as of now, GCHQ is shut down, and so all we are doing is monitoring radio traffic. As you know, our defences are as good as it gets, and this thing went straight through them like a hot knife through butter."

John felt that he'd better support this very welcome intervention. "Whatever this thing is," he said, "it uses software to travel. Passwords and encryption systems are software, and it isn't blocked by them; it uses them to *pass through*."

The general had gone a little pale. He suddenly pushed his seat back, turned to the PM, and said, "Please excuse me, Prime Minister. I had better act quickly on what I have just been told. I won't be long." He then hurriedly exited the room.

"So, Professor," the PM sighed, turning back to John. "How far is this going to spread? How much damage are we talking about?"

"Everywhere and everything, Prime Minister," John replied. "It's already happening. It seemed to have started with what we call 'legacy software'; essentially, old stuff that should have been replaced years ago, but appears to have evolved quickly and is attacking much more modern software languages. It must be in pretty much everything by now. In fact, the satellite systems are probably toast, and it won't be long before it hits the mobile phone network, too."

At this point, the door opened, and a secretary came in, quickly making her way down the table toward the PM, offering her a note. The room went quiet whilst she read it.

"Quite a prediction, Professor," she said after a moment. "It seems we are experiencing quite some chaos with shipping in the channel and aircraft in the air. The GPS system has died."

"Our lives are run by algorithms, Prime Minister," John said, shrugging. "Quite a large percentage of the population doesn't even know what an algorithm is, but they pretty much run everything these days, including most of your government departments. This, then, is an algorithm *plague*. It will take us back in time. Lyons tea houses were the first to use a computerised wages system in 1951. No computers back then; no commercial jets, no GPS navigation. That's the age we'll be returning to. Only this time, there'll be no local bank branches and an economy that doesn't use cash."

"How can this have *happened*?" asked the PM in disbelief.

"Simple, really," replied John, a bit more boldly. "With the internet, once we linked everything up worldwide, we also *exposed* everything worldwide. We have rushed headlong into the biggest social experiment in history, and we have all welcomed it with open arms because it seemed so clever, convenient, and efficient. It was a magic way for the banks to cut costs. And for the government to do the same, for that matter. No one has ever questioned it despite its obvious problems and failings, and we have left ourselves wide open to this. It was just a matter of time, if you ask me."

"But I thought you guys were monitoring the internet and protecting people from hackers and criminals. Wasn't that your role for us?" asked the PM.

"A rear-guard action, Prime Minister. All we can do is play electronic ping pong, essentially. If we see something coming, we try to bat it back. This ball is completely invisible, and with respect to the prime minister, it's the politicians who have, let's say, 'weaponised' software. I am not saying this problem has come from any particular country, but the attack on the NHS some time ago was based on 'weaponised' software that leaked from America's NSA. So, once you start down that track, there isn't much someone like me can do."

It was safe to say at this point that the meeting was a strange and tense one. John could not have predicted how much of it would be composed of a one-on-one talk with the prime minister herself. And yet here they were.

"So, let me try and summarise what you are saying, Professor," said the PM, after another uneasy silence and some murmuring. "We are faced with a sort of social Armageddon. No bombs dropped, but no money left. That is, apart from what we have in our pockets. No trade possible. And the economy is not so much in trouble as it is nonexistent. And there is no obvious way out for the immediate future?"

"I think that sums things up reasonably well," said John. "You haven't seen the worst of it quite yet though. In practical terms, the NHS will be in trouble, and most government departments, especially the treasury, will be..." he paused whilst he tried to think of a suitable word. "...paralysed," he finished.

"Great," said the PM, leaning back in her chair. "I have only been in office three months, and now this." No one laughed.

"Okay," she then said, leaning forward once more and intertwining her fingers. "Let us go around the table, department by department. I want positive, practical suggestions. Stuart, could you get us started, please?" She gestured to a typical grey male civil servant – grey suit, white shirt, blue tie, grey hair. Stuart was from the Department for Business, Energy, and Industrial Strategy, as it turned out.

"Can you keep the lights on and the central heating working?" she asked him.

"Possibly," came Stuart's noncommittal reply. "Obviously, the system relies quite a lot on computer control systems. So, if the engineers can jury rig the stations so they can run safely, and we are not concerned with anyone paying for the power output, then we can likely manage. I suppose a lot of industry will come to a grinding halt, so capacity should not be an issue, but energy may be. We will have to close down the nuclear power stations, for a certainty, as they are too dependent on computer control. I believe that is already happening. The situation with regard to petrol and diesel is less clear at the moment. We will have to arrange for essential services to be supplied and public transport from the emergency supply. That way, we can have some renewable energy sources, but to be honest, they don't amount to much. Therefore, the big question is, 'Can we keep the gas flowing?' And at the moment, I haven't a clue."

"Better go and find out then," said the PM breezily, gesturing for Stuart to leave the room – he did. "And that directs us to Allen at transport."

A slightly scruffy man wearing a kippah gave a heavy shrug in response. "I, um. I am going to make a suggestion, Prime Minister, if I may…?"

"Of course. All ears, Allen."

"Well, I am going to suggest that in this crisis… and no one has yet mentioned the words 'state of emergency' yet, that we keep all public transport running for free. I apologise if this sounds like some big communist proposal, but people simply won't have any money for petrol and they will still have to be able to move around, right? The ports and airports will be in chaos for some time… We have told the air control people to ground everything as soon as possible, though I believe this wasn't fast enough, and, well, there are problems brewing. Shipping is probably as dangerous as aviation; most modern ships are a big tub with a propeller and a computer, and they navigate by GPS… I have no idea what will happen if they lose the computer *or* the GPS."

"Okay," said the PM, cutting off the anxious man. "Suggestion noted for action. Next, Helen. Tell me about communications, would you?"

Helen was a woman in her mid-fifties with grey hair and a modest weight problem from the Department of Culture, Media and Sport. With a look of distress on her face, she said, "I haven't a clue at the moment, Prime Minister. I believe the landline system is immune and pretty well bulletproof. I will have to talk to the BBC, though, and see what they can provide. Presumably, radio will be okay, but… I cannot comment yet on TV. If we lose the internet and satellite transmission, we may well be back in the 1950s, as Professor Davenport has said, with terrestrial only. But how many channels, and whether they can work without computers… I simply don't know."

"Alright," said the PM, "On your way, then. Go and find out what you can and report back. Thomas, the NHS?"

Next up, a thin, rather pale man of indeterminate age in a neat pin-striped suit gave yet another shrug. He reminded John of Eeyore from *Winnie the Pooh*. "Lord only knows, Prime Minister. We had started to look at contingency plans after the last debacle, but we will now have to introduce as much of that as we can. I think we have to assume that the NHS computer system is stuffed. I suppose the roads won't be as crowded for ambulances, at least. But the poor dears won't know where they are going without sat nav."

"Thank you, Thomas," said the PM, shifting her gaze to the man seated next to him. "I will come to you in a moment, General, but first I want to know about food, if that's alright." She then made eye contact with a middle-aged woman who sat opposite John. "Lady Arbuthnot, what can you tell us?" she asked the startled woman.

The words "Designer Oxfam" sprang into John's mind as he looked at her in a rather excentric collection of various bits of clothing, and he had to suppress a giggle. He realised that the tension and nerves were getting to him, but when she began speaking, it was in a rather beautiful, well-modulated voice full of natural authority – not what John had expected.

"As you know, Prime Minister," she started, "at any given time, we have enough food available to feed the nation for about three days. After that, we are up the proverbial creek without said paddle. I will likely wind up the WI, the WRVS, the Salvation Army, and the YMCA. Not to mention the food bank organisations and the religious organisations. From there, we can start setting up soup kitchens as soon as possible."

"Soup kitchens?" repeated the PM.

"Yes, Prime Minister," confirmed Lady Arbuthnot. "Quite a large proportion of the population cannot feed themselves. If they cannot buy takeaways or ready meals because they have no money, they will starve to death. You can forget rationing of food as such. If you gave these people a ration card, it would have to be for pizzas, burgers, fish and chips, and so on. In fact, that may be an option we have to look at. If you do call a state of emergency, we may have to requisition McDonald's."

In the instant she said it, everyone took it to be a joke and started to lightly giggle. When it became clear that she wasn't joking, a sobering silence fell on the table.

"The point is, we will have to sort out a form of rationing, Prime Minister," said Lady Arbuthnot. "The country cannot produce enough food for everyone. If shipping is not available without navigation aids, then our only supply line will be the Channel Tunnel. But as for how we pay for imports, I will leave that to you."

The PM looked grim for a moment before looking back toward the general. "So, General, what about the armed forces?"

The general, who had only just returned to his seat took a moment to respond, looking down at the table with a furrowed brow. "Presumably," he began, "you will want us to take to the streets to support the civil authorities in order to provide security and to stop any looting. Right, Prime Minister?"

She didn't respond.

"Well, we can help with feeding people, too, of course," continued the general. "We have field kitchens and stocks of rations for our soldiers. And by the sound of it, we are not going to be much use at defending the nation if the Navy cannot navigate and the RAF cannot fly.

"Thank you, General," said the PM, finally. "We can talk after the meeting, and we can discuss a mobilisation."

She then turned her attention to the table at large. "Well, ladies and gentlemen, it seems obvious I will have to declare a state of emergency."

"You may have to declare martial law," added the general.

"Possibly," said the PM, quickly, as if the thought were already in the back of her mind. "But I will keep that in reserve for now, until we know how the public is going to react."

The room went quiet again as the PM sat still, tapping at the table with her pen. After a few moments, she took a deep breath and said, "Has anyone any idea as to how we can get out of this mess without it really becoming Armageddon? And please, I don't want the usual reticence to commit. We are *beyond* that, I'd say."

No one said anything for some time, and so the PM sat it out, letting the deafening silence pile on the pressure. "Fair enough," she said sharply under her breath.

"I have one suggestion to make, Prime Minister," John found himself saying, suddenly. And why not? He wasn't a hardened civil servant, and he was cursed with a pretty creative mind and an engineer's need to solve problems. "But I'll warn you, it *is* pretty screwy."

"I don't care how screwy it is," the PM responded with a sad smile. "Let's hear it."

"Well," said John, "It, er, seems to me we have to return to a cash economy as soon as we can. But we don't actually have very much cash in circulation. Nor do we have a banking system that is designed to handle it. On top of that, no one has a usable bank account anymore. So, my suggestion is this: We revalue. We divide the price of everything by 100 and give everyone £5."

The room had somehow grown even quieter than before, John reckoned.

The PM eyed John blankly for a moment, then looked over at the guy from the Bank of England and raised an eyebrow, prompting him to speak on the matter at hand.

"Well, um," he began, fretfully. "Everyone would have to do this worldwide, Prime Minister. For it to, um, *work*."

"Go on," said the prime minister.

"The scope for criminal activity would be enormous, but if we can't return to electronic banking in the immediate future, then we have to find a way to get commerce and trade started again. So, an idea like this may actually be the only thing we can do. At any given time, the amount of cash in circulation is considerably less than 10% of the amount of money in circulation, and that is reflected to some extent by what the banks hold in cash. I mean, it's more complicated than that, but as a rough approximation, it fits. Presumably, to make it work, the divider would have to be a simple round number; 100 might do it. But you will have to convince the US *and* the EU to do the same thing. And we'd have to figure out some way to make it work with our existing currency for now until new notes and coins can be issued."

"So, not a *completely* stupid idea then?" asked the prime minister, eyebrow raised once more.

"Oh no," came the response. "It's possibly the only way out."

"In that case," said the prime minister, tapping her pen enthusiastically on the table, "you and the treasury can go get your heads together and turn the professor's suggestion into an easy-to-understand strategy that I can try and sell as soon as humanly possible."

She then looked over at John. "Thank you, Professor Davenport. If this idea works, I will reserve you a seat in the Lords."

John smiled at her awkwardly, unsure if he should say anything.

"Now, I need to go and call a state of emergency," she declared to the table. "And you all need to start preparing for one. I am going to ask the professor here to help coordinate the UK's attempts to figure out what the hell this is. And then swiftly kill it, of course. He can then liaise with GCHQ with regard to trying to identify where it came from. Now, I realise that MI6, Special Branch, and MI5 will have a finger in this pie, but I don't want him spending all his time answering their questions, do you understand? So, please, you two stay in touch and GCHQ can talk to the rest of them, got it?"

The two men in question looked at each other, then back at the PM, and nodded.

"Good," she said, rising from her spot. "Well, we all have a lot to do. There is one point we should try and verify if we can. Professor Davenport, you said that if this were a cyber-attack, then presumably the country that initiated it would be immune. Is there any way of checking out that hypothesis?"

Before John could answer, a person from GCHQ came to his rescue. "It is an interesting suggestion, Prime Minister. And we will certainly try and check it out, but it will have been a deeply stupid thing to do.

Even if their systems are still working, they will be next to useless. Furthermore, they will be totally isolated from any commerce and trade."

"Fair enough," responded the PM, "But if this is a cyber-attack, whoever did it will pay a price." And with that, she left.

Without the PM, the meeting was seemingly all but wrapped up. However, the remaining people present clearly felt less restrained and began talking a bit more freely. The guy from the Bank of England told John that he had hit the nail on the head with his £5 solution. "It could be another generation before we get back to electronic money again," he told John.

After that, the guy from GCHQ came up to John and asked him if he had any other ideas about what they could do to stop this thing.

"Well, we are going to see if we can invite it into a sort of electronic cul-de-sac where we can trap it and examine it," John said with a shrug. "At least, that's the idea. But even if we are successful, we then have to analyse it and find a way to kill it. There's likely a worldwide race going on when it comes to this. But the thing is, it's bound to be too late. At this rate, there won't be much operational software left."

They looked at each other solemnly for a moment, and the man nodded. "Well, good luck anyway," he said. "I won't have a job until you succeed, and no doubt the politicians will want me up and running again as soon as possible. That said, to be honest with you, there may not be much left out there for me to monitor. It will be back to listening in to radio signals. Not my bag, really."

"I would get down to your nearest library and see if they can dig out a book on Morse code, if I were you," quipped John.

The two burst out laughing, which felt good after such a tense afternoon. Everyone looked at them as though they were insane, and perhaps for the moment, they were a little. Whatever their lives had been up until this point, they were bound to change completely along with almost everyone else's on the planet. And, as John decided to himself as he exited the building, you could either laugh or cry.

The Texel Adventurer—Zero + 10hrs

Michael Straver shut the toilet door behind him and stepped forward onto the bridge of his ship, the Texel Adventurer. The view from the bridge was a sight that never failed to thrill him, even after hundreds of days spent here. She was a fairly new 20,000 TEU container ship weighing over 200,000 tonnes. She could hold 20,000 twenty-foot equivalent units (TEUs), which was an enormous amount of goods. Michael didn't worry about it too much, though. As a pragmatic Netherlander, he wasn't given to too many flights of fancy.

Instead, he stepped over to his central position and checked the ECDIS, or electronic display and information system. This was a large screen that generated a naval chart showing the position of the ship, its heading, and its speed. The chart also showed the depth of water they were sailing in and the contours of the sea bed. In front of this was the main workstation of the bridge.

The ship largely sailed itself, behaving rather like a giant robot, with the bridge acting as its brain. In fact, Michael had read an article recently about the new robotic ships being developed in Norway. His crew totaled 13, but these new ships were crewless. For Michael, it was a slightly unnerving thought.

On her way to Michael's home port of Rotterdam, the Texel Adventurer was sailing off the French coast, about 20 miles from Calais. It was a fine day – the sea was calm and pretty clear, apart from a massive oil tanker a mile or so ahead. As Michael eyed it in the distance, he thought of how excited he was to see his wife and children later that night.

Just then, the ECDIS screen went blank. Michael stared at the screen in confusion. This had never happened before. He initiated the backup screen, but soon enough, it did the same thing. He then noticed that the radar screens and every other visual display unit on the bridge followed suit. Just like that, everything had gone black.

His feelings of well-being evaporated instantly, and as he did his best not to replace them with panic, he heard the worst sound he could possibly imagine, *silence*. His ship should never be silent. Silence meant disaster. It meant the twin MAN, seven-cylinder diesel engines that supplied over 70,000 bhp and could push the ship along at the most economical speed of 15 knots had stopped.

They were adrift. No steerage, no control. *Nothing*. Michael wasn't panicking now; he just felt numb. But he wasn't alone on the bridge. His six-foot, four-inch deck officer, Johannes Oostrom, brought him back to reality with a string of expletives. Michael wasn't a fan of foul language on the bridge; he thought it was unprofessional. But on this occasion, he was happy to give Johannes some slack. They looked at one another with stunned expressions and turned in unison as the door to the bridge burst open and the chief engineer marched straight up to the now dead main panel. More expletives followed.

Michael's chief engineer was a Brit called James Harkness. They were all of a similar age – in their late 30s – and all pretty tech savvy. However, none of them had ever envisaged being in this position. True, they had trained for emergencies, knew how to abandon ship if need be, and were well aware that the sea could be an extremely dangerous place. These men had been through plenty of storms and high seas and had handled many situations with calm assurance and professionalism, but this? To have nothing, no computers, no engines, no power, nothing at all to work with? This was simply *horrible*.

"Okay," said James, "this has got to do with the virus they're all talking about."

"*Virus*? What virus?" asked Michael, wide-eyed.

"I was watching the news in the mess room this morning," explained James. "They're saying the banking system is collapsing worldwide and loads of other software systems are dying. Something has infected the internet and is killing software at a mad pace. That's what the media's saying, anyway. They're normally pretty dim when it comes to anything technical, though, so there aren't many details."

"My God..." mumbled Johannes.

"I see," was all Michael managed to say. After a pause, he asked the million-dollar question: "Can you get us going again?"

"Jesus!" said James. "That's a rotten question to ask. Let me think for a minute?"

So, Michael and Johannes stood there and let James think. In his own head, Michael wasn't too worried about the prospect of anyone on board being hurt or dying. After all, they had a perfectly good lifeboat they could launch off the back of the ship, and in these conditions, they could sail it anywhere they wanted. But giving the order to abandon ship was rather daunting. And what about all that stuff out there in the containers? And that was to say nothing of his beloved ship, his job, or the company he worked for. They all depended on the software doing its job.

As the three men continued to stand there awkwardly, it occurred to Michael that he had better talk to the crew first and then contact the French Coast Guard. There was no immediate danger, but they deserved to know as soon as possible. So, whilst James kept on thinking, Michael switched on the ship's speaker system – which thankfully had a backup battery supply – and explained the situation as best as he could to the rest of the crew. He told them to get together in the mess room and wait for further updates. After that, he called up the Coast Guard on the radio and explained their position.

"You are the fifth ship to call in so far in the same position," the Coast Guard told him. "All our computers are also dead. We don't think our helicopters will be able to fly, and our radar screens are down. So, there's not much we can do to help, unfortunately."

"Okay," said James, finally finishing his thinking. "We have to isolate the ship from the outside. In a sense, it is already, as we have no power, but we need to turn off the satellite link to make sure. Luckily, that's easily done. Then, I think we'll need to disconnect all the computers in the main panels here on the bridge; they must all be contaminated. We have a spare engine management unit, so I will go and dig that out and replace the present one in the engine room. From there, we will have to try and run the ship from a bridge wing unit, which has been turned off, so they should be isolated and not contaminated. You won't have the ECDIS, so you will have to use paper charts and dead reckoning. Also, we won't have radar, but we should have power, and so we should be able to steer the ship still. We have the magnetic and possibly the gyro compass, and as long as we can see where we are going, we should be able to make it to Rotterdam."

James took a deep breath after that, a small smile forming on his face.

"I do love an optimist," said Michael, impressed. "But how long is this going to take?"

James sighed, his smile disappearing.

"Well," he began, "get the other guys up from the mess room to disconnect this lot, and I'll go and change the EMU... It shouldn't take more than an hour."

"Okay, great," said Michael. "Go past the mess room on your way down, pick out who you need, and tell them what you want. I'll radio the Coast Guard again and give them an update." Michael hoped he sounded confident, but he still felt pretty shaky.

An hour later, after James had double-checked everything, they set about starting the engines. It was no simple task; you didn't just turn the ignition switch or press a button. You needed to pump high-pressure air from big, compressed air tanks into the pistons in order to push them around. It was always a slightly nerve-wracking process, and this time it had everyone on edge, especially as the engines had not been closed down in a controlled way.

But diesels are nothing if not robust, and the EMU was giving out the right signals to the fuel injectors. And so, the massive engines finally kicked in, which was just as well because the ship had been drifting towards the oil tanker, which had also conked out. In short, it was beginning to get too close for comfort.

Michael contacted the Coast Guard with the news that they were underway again and then passed the radio to James so that he could tell them exactly what he had done. The Coast Guard had several other ships within radio range that were able to listen in and take notes. Some said they thought they could try and do the same thing, whilst others said they didn't have spare EMUs on board, so there was quite a bit of discussion about where they might be had and if it would be possible to get them out to the ships. With a lot of calm professionalism and centuries of unwritten laws of the sea, ships got going, ships dropped anchor, and ships had tows. And ships ran aground. Life's never perfect.

Rotterdam

The trip through the Strait of Dover had been a surreal experience; it had become apparent that all the newer, larger vessels were in trouble, whilst, at the very least, a lot of the older and smaller ships seemed to be under control.

Michael had spoken to the Coast Guard about offering a tow to anyone in distress, but the Coast Guard captain felt the Texel Adventurer was simply too big to try any heroic moves in the channel. As he told Michael, he would prefer it if the Texel made it further out into the sea, allowing more room for the other helpless and drifting vessels scattered all about.

James, the engineer on board the Texel, was meanwhile talking on the radio until his voice gave out. He had explained all he'd done to get the ship moving again, and how his efforts had undoubtedly helped a great many ships – at least the ones that had the spares on board to follow his lead.

A few miles out from Rotterdam, they came across a coastal supply tanker that was adrift and managed to get a tow rope across. As they reached the entrance to Rotterdam, they had to let the tanker drift free into the Hook of Holland, where it could drop anchor along with dozens of other ships. It would be safe there, and the crew could use the ship's boats to get ashore to reach help and get some instructions. They had managed to get the auxiliary generator working, and as such, they had power for the lights, heating, and some of the deck equipment. In short, they could manage for a while.

With a degree of difficulty, Michael positioned the Texel Adventurer in line with the entrance to the port and headed for the Maasvlakte container port. As he did so, he radioed to the port authority to let them know the Texel was coming and to ask which dock to head for. When asked if they needed any tugs, Michael declined, suggesting they had good control of the ship and that he could use his bow and stern thrusters; his only problem was that he would have to dock the ship himself rather than let the computer do it. Fortunately, the port authority told him they could send over a pilot to help. Michael thanked them profusely and felt the stress leave his body. Some tugs would have been great, but he wasn't sure how he would have paid for them. He was trained to dock the ship; he had even done the course at Warsash Maritime Academy in the UK, sailing scale model ships. Of course, back then, the ship more or less docked itself with the help of GPS and the computer control system. Now, it was entirely up to him. The pilot would help, and for that he was relieved – but he knew it was still his ship and his responsibility.

It took what felt like ages, but eventually, the Texel Adventurer was safely docked, in the right position. Michael and the pilot disembarked and headed for the office block across the unloading bay that housed the port authority offices.

The experience was a strange one. Normally, the place was a hive of activity, but on this particular evening, it was quiet. There was a complete absence of activity, and it felt weird. Michael found out more when he went to see the dock manager, Aaron de Vries. Michael and Aaron knew each other quite well on a professional level. And in Michael's view, Aaron had always come across as a very calm and well organised individual. He was quite tall, being born and bred in Holland, and as he cycled to work and back most days, he was quite fit, too. But on this occasion, he looked worn out and a little grey.

"Well done for getting here safely," he said, shaking Michael's hand. "I hear your engineer deserves a medal. That fix he came up with has helped quite a few ships, it seems."

The two men sat down in Aaron's office, looking a little messier than Michael had remembered it.

"That's good to know," said Michael. "Can you bring me up to speed on what's been happening on the mainland? We've been a bit preoccupied for some time now, and we had our satellite link turned off."

"Well, where to start?" laughed Aaron. "We are totally wiped out at the moment, my friend. As you know, this dock was fully automated, and, well. We were too slow to stop the Plague."

"The *what?*" asked Michael.

"The *Plague*, Michael. It's what everyone is calling it. The 'Algorithm Plague.' It isn't a scam or some sort of hacker's thing; no one seems to be getting any richer off it. It just sort of destroys software, kills algorithms, and uses the internet to infect systems. In your case, it came into your ship via the satellite connection you had to the web and killed all the software on any of the ship's computers you had turned on. Honestly, it was a stroke of genius on the part of that engineer of yours to do what he did. Sealing off the ship and the dead computers, and only using a kit that had not been turned on? *Genius.*"

Michael was almost speechless. "Have they figured out where it came from?" he finally asked Michael, suddenly wondering if it really even mattered.

"No, don't think so," Aaron said sadly. "They have only just managed to avoid a third world war by realising that everyone has been hit equally badly. Word is the Americans were all set to blame the Russians, and vice versa… but then each found out that the other had been just as wrecked."

Michael sat back in his chair, his head in his hands.

"I need to get home," said Aaron after a pause. "But I wanted to wait until you docked to explain that we won't be unloading your ship anytime soon. We're going to have to figure out a way to do it manually. And even then, we have nowhere to send you containers, no staff to handle them, and no money to pay any if we did. The banks are gone. Kaput. Disappeared. No money, no transactions, no *nothing.*"

Both men sat there in exhausted defeat for a minute.

Finally, Michael asked, "Can I use your phone to let my wife know I'm okay?"

"Of course," said Aaron, gesturing to his landline. "If I were you, I would tell her to expect you home tomorrow morning. It's late now, and transport is difficult, as you could imagine.

"Before I forget, Michael, can I suggest you launch one of your boats?" he asked.

"What for?"

"Well, we're asking all the ships that are docked to help us guard them. The world is full of idiots right about now, and some of them are taking matters into their own hands. They think this place is packed with goodies to steal, so we are having to increase our security. Don't worry, we won't expect your crew to fight anyone off, but it's a big area to watch, so the more the merrier. If they see anything, our security guys will deal with it, and as you're helping us, we can keep your boat supplied with fuel, of course. You'll be able to use the boat to get home tomorrow and drop any crew you can spare in Rotterdam."

"Okay," said Michael. "That's no problem. I will have to call my company manager and see what we can do about the ship. Trouble is, I don't have his home number. I don't suppose there will be anyone in the main office?"

"Does he live in Rotterdam?" asked Aaron.

"Ringvaartweg."

"Ah, nice," said Aaron, smiling. "Well, you can try looking him up in the directory, but if he lives in a swanky area like that, he will probably be ex-directory. It may be worth trying your office. They might have someone there taking calls and messages, and most of the shipping companies are in trouble in one way or another. Right about now, there are bound to be hundreds of cruise ships stuck out at sea with no power."

Michael was silent for a moment, contemplating those words. "All those people," he finally said, "and not a working toilet between them."

The two men looked at each other gravely for a moment and then burst out laughing.

"Oh dear," said Aaron, drying his eyes. "That isn't very charitable of us, is it? I think I must be feeling a bit hysterical."

"Oh, no," said Michael. "You just don't like cruise ship captains; it's quite normal."

With that, the two fell about laughing once more.

"Alright, alright," Michael said finally, taking a breath and coming to his senses. "I need to call my wife. After that, I'll call the office. Is there anything I can tell them other than that we're here and safe?"

"I really don't think so," replied Aaron, shrugging. "For now, all this is over. Your ship will have a typical cargo, let me see… a bit less than half a mixture of stuff. The rest is household stuff: appliances, toys, furniture, textiles, and car parts. No one has any money or any credit to buy any of that. If you have any foodstuffs, like rice or tinned food, then the government might want it once we've figured out a way to get the cranes to work. But as far as I can see, your ship, along with all the others, is going to be going nowhere for a long time. It's anyone's guess at the moment what sort of banking system we will eventually be able to patch together. No doubt you have some Malaysian crew members?"

Michael looked up and nodded.

"Well, they won't be able to get home until the planes are flying again, and lord only knows how long that will take. At least for now, they have somewhere to stay and something to eat; I assume you have enough stores on board for some time?"

Again, Michael nodded.

"Okay, well, we will arrange a power supply for the ship and a land line so they can phone home. That said, they're welcome to come to the office and use this phone, too. My staff will help them as much as they can. I'm going to head home now, but I will be back first thing tomorrow. You make your calls and come and see me before you go home tomorrow, okay?"

"Of course," said Michael. "Thanks, Aaron. I truly appreciate all this."

Aaron stood up and shook his friend's hand. "You did well today, Michael. It may not change what the future has in store, but you can hold the memory and feel proud of it."

Michael felt more relieved than proud, and now that the pressure was off, profoundly tired, to boot. However, he managed to phone his wife and tell her that he was safe and sound and that he would be getting home sometime tomorrow. She had a lot to tell him in response, but sensed he was more than a little worn out and thus opted to only ask him how he was going to get home. She wouldn't be able to get him – there wasn't enough petrol in the car.

Michael explained to her the situation with the lifeboats. "I will get one of the guys to bring me home in one of those," he promised. "Though I'm not sure how long it may take. I may have to come back and sort out what we are going to do with the ship. But we'll be together no matter what, okay?"

They wished each other a heartfelt goodnight before hanging up.

As he reflected on the call, Michael realised it hadn't been the greatest on his part, but he knew it was the best he could accomplish for now. Next, he called his company's office number and was surprised to find that the phone was answered promptly. As it appeared, they must have managed a rota to keep the reception manned 24/7 in case they got precisely the sort of call Michael was making. They were able to give him the number for his CEO, Karl van den Berg, who also answered promptly.

"Hello, Sir," said Michael. "It's Michael Straver of the Texel Adventurer. We are docked here at Rotterdam."

"Hi Michael, it's good to hear from you," Van der Berg responded. "Well done for getting the ship home safely. Is everyone okay?"

"Yes, we are all fine, Sir. A bit tired and not sure what happens next, but we're okay."

"Good, good," said Van der Berg. "What has the dock manager told you?"

"He says there's not much he can do at the moment. All his computers are out, and he cannot run the cranes, but they are working on that, so as to access any food we may have on board. I need to check the manifest when I get back. Fortunately, my chief officer always insists on printing off a copy, so we can look through the miscellaneous section and check out what we have. He's asked us to launch one of the boats so that we can help run a patrol of the dock. He'll keep us topped up with fuel in exchange. I was also planning on going home tomorrow for a while."

"That sounds like a good idea, Michael. As long as it doesn't put any of the crew at risk, I see no issue with that."

"The dock manager says not, at least," replied Michael. "He just wants eyes out there who can report to their security people. It's no doubt a sensible precaution, but the dock is a long way from anywhere."

"Not by boat it isn't, Michael," came Van der Berg's voice over the phone. "But I think the police are patrolling regularly, so it should be okay. And if the port operators can't unload the ships, your average yobbo will stand no chance. I don't know what to tell you for the immediate future, however. As a company, we exist in name only, like everyone else. We don't have a bank account anymore, so even if we had money, we would have no way to pay it out. You have some cash in the ship's safe, right?"

"I believe so, Sir, yes."

"Well, if you want to give some to any of the crew to see them safely home, that'll be up to you. But the Malaysian guys are stuck here until planes start flying again. I take it you have enough supplies to stay with the ship for a while?"

"Yes, we are okay for a week or two, I think," said Michael, pondering this for a moment. "That's something else I need to check."

"Of course," said Van den Berg. "That's fine, Michael. Go get some rest. Go and see your wife, check out your supplies, and we will get together in a few days' time to look at the situation properly. I have no doubt the politicians will want to get trade going again as soon as possible, but my guess is the global economy is dead in the water for now. In fact, capitalism as we know it is either dead or very badly wounded. So, the ship will likely stay right where she is for quite some time."

After their goodbyes, Michael went back to the ship and got all the crew together in the mess. When they were all settled, he told them what little information he knew to get them up to speed.

"First of all, guys, you can go ashore in pairs and use the phone in the dock manager's office to call home," Michael announced. "I'll let you decide when you want to do that, as it is getting rather late. It's been a long day, so I won't keep you. We all need some rest, but we will need to keep watch, too, so if you are okay with the rota as it stands, let's continue with it. We'll be here for some time, it sounds like. For those of you who would normally have to fly home, I'm sorry to say, but there simply isn't anything flying anywhere in the world now. Furthermore, I have no idea how long it will be before planes can take off again. The government is keeping public transport and the trains running, but to what extent I don't know, so we'll need to wait for more information. The dock manager wants us to launch one of our boats so that we can help patrol the harbour. In exchange, he will keep us topped up with fuel, so I am going to suggest we launch one in the morning and go into Rotterdam. From there, we can drop a couple of you off in the centre and I can go and see my family whilst you have a prowl around and see what's happening. We have enough stores on board to be comfortable for some time, but it might be a good idea to start looking over what we have and reducing rations a bit to make them last longer. Anyway, let's get some sleep for now, and tomorrow we can get out and gather some information. With that, God willing, we can work out a plan."

And with that, Michael went back to his cabin, allowed himself a stiff drink, and crashed out on his bunk.

The following morning, they launched a lifeboat into the dock. Some ships had a single lifeboat on a chute at the ship's stern, but the Texel had two on either side of the bridge complex, about one-third of the way down the ship from the bow. It was a Day-Glo orange, fully enclosed motorboat with an inboard marine diesel, seats, and enough supplies to last several days at sea.

After much debate, it was decided that amongst these supplies would be one of the shotguns the crew used for clay pigeon shooting off the ship's stern. Michael wasn't too happy about this at first but given the unprecedented situation they had found themselves in, everyone agreed a little self-defence couldn't hurt. Michael's only insistence was that the gun was stored away out of sight. Also included in the supplies were two large Hold-Alls from the ship's cook. These contained coffee, tea, sugar, dried milk, rice, flour, dried yeast, salt, tinned meat and stew, and toilet rolls. According to the radio, these were all in short supply.

Michael had to go to the dock office again to call his wife. Once he had her on the phone, he asked her to meet him down by the river with the beach cart they kept stored in the garage.

With everything assembled on board, Michael set out from the dock, along with Johannes and James, leaving two of the crew's Malaysian deck ratings behind to guard the ship.

The lifeboat made its way across the mouth of the port entrance and into the Nieuwe Waterweg Ship Canal and then along the Het Scheur past the principality of Rosenburg and finally into the Nieuwe Maas – the modern central area of the city of Rotterdam. He dropped Johannes and James off at Het Park and arranged to pick them up there later in the day.

They had seen plenty of people on the riverside as the boat travelled up, and as this was Holland, almost everyone was unsurprisingly riding a bike. The lack of cars and petrol certainly made the city quieter, but it hadn't stopped people getting out and about, which Michael thought was a delight to see. The river traffic was light and almost every berth was occupied, so it had been a bit tricky dropping the guys off, and the Day-Glo orange boat drew some curious glances from locals, but the trip still managed to be a peaceful and uneventful one. The boat carried on under the city's bridges, including the spectacular Erasmusbrug, past the island of Noordereiland and around the "S" bends of the river until they came to a fork and turned left into the Hollandsche Ijssel to head for Krimpen aan den Ijssel. This was where Michael lived with his wife and young daughter.

The lifeboat turned right into the canal and headed for a street that connected the Haven to the main *parallelweg*, where Michael had arranged to meet his wife. They had to moor alongside a couple of barges and cross over them to get to the shore where, much to Michael's surprise, his wife and several other people stood around an SUV with its bonnet up.

She waved when she spotted him and ran over to give him a big bear hug. It took a few minutes to sort out that she had been given a lift in a neighbour's car, which was a plug-in hybrid with a battery range of about 70 miles. As Michael's wife and the neighbour had been waiting for half an hour or so, and as there was little to do in the meantime, they had begun talking with some of the local bargees, and before very long, the bonnet had been lifted up on the car so that the more mechanically minded could peer in at the hybrid setup. The neighbour had a charge point set up at home, and as electricity was free at the moment, it wasn't a problem for him to take people to the hospital or the doctors' office and, of course, pick up the trickle of returnees like Michael. Michael knew the man by sight and thanked him sincerely for the lift by giving him a couple of toilet rolls.

It was a huge relief to be home and to see that his wife and daughter were both safe and well. The food items were welcome, but they could get a meal at their local kitchen with a ration of milk, some bread, and a bit of butter. There was also talk of opening the schools again soon.

Michael would have loved to have been able to stay longer, but that would have to wait until he had sorted out what was going to happen to the ship and his crew. So, after a couple of hours at home and the promise that he would be back again tomorrow, he got his bike out from the garage and set off back to where he had left the lifeboat. The crew had been chatting to the barges, and so by the time they had picked up the other crew members and returned to the ship, they all had a much better idea as to what was happening ashore.

The crew all gathered together in the mess for an evening meal and to pool all that they now knew. It seemed that all of the governments across Europe had realised that the best way to keep the peace for now was to make sure everyone had power and at least some access to public transport. Keeping the power system working was a must, as this ensured that they had water, and with manufacturing, banks, and retail establishments closed, the demand for power was a fraction of what it normally was. Trains, buses, and trams were all running, but for now, aircraft were grounded, just as had been rumoured. Planes had been grounded very early, though not early enough in some cases, where they had fallen out of the sky. No one really knew yet how many lives had been lost, but it would be some time before some sort of safe system could be established.

The biggest problem, undeniably, was money. For now, the power, transport, and landline telephone systems were entirely free. Food at the feeding stations that had been set up in each neighbourhood was free, as well. What food there was had been sequestered by the government, and the army and government organisations had access to fuel in order to transport what was needed to keep people alive. However, everyone was still waiting to see what could be done about the collapse of the banking system. Apart from that, it seemed there was no television for now, but radios worked, and there was some hope that a limited terrestrial TV system would be up and running soon.

Shipping was generally in chaos, with the main concern being cruise ships and oil tankers. People had been arriving in places in lifeboats all over the world as cruise ships had been abandoned at sea. It had also been found that helicopters that had been turned off when the plague hit were still okay, and that there were still lots of small aircraft that were safe to fly. As such, some limited searches had taken place, and some ships and tankers had been rescued, but there were still a lot missing.

The general consensus amongst the crew of the Texel Adventurer was that they should stay with the ship for now in order to see how things developed. Michael and Johannes could go home for now, and those aboard the ship could get in touch if ever they needed them. James, the engineer, had spoken to his parents, and they were both fine and thought he would probably be better off staying with his ship than trying to trek home now.

And so, with everything arranged, Michael had another night aboard and then went home the following day to his family.

Dorothy—Zero + 48hrs

Dorothy, or "Dot," as everyone called her, finished clearing up after breakfast and decided she would go up and see how Caroline was managing. The last two days had been particularly strange, and she felt like doing something that would seem normal. Grabbing her handbag and setting off to catch the bus would feel as close to normal as anything else, she figured.

Dot lived in a sandstone terraced house in a small Lancashire cotton town, but it was by no means a "mean" little house, as some may have thought. Dot's home had been built to house a mill manager rather than a worker, and as such, it was quite nice. It was situated at the end of a terrace and had gardens at the front, back, and side. Its rooms were generous in size, too, with a big bay window in the living room, overlooking the street.

She was a small and fit woman, and this was due to the near constant activities she got up to from the moment she woke up in the morning to the moment she went to bed at night. Dot could drive but preferred to walk and use the bus, and her husband typically used their only car to commute to work. Dot's husband was a bus driver when she met him some 30 years ago, but he was an intelligent fellow and managed to work his way up to be the local area transport manager through various changes in the business.

The couple had two sons in their early 20s, both still at home but both with decent jobs. Dot wanted them to go off and get married and set up homes of their own, but nonetheless, they were nice lads and were used to living in a quiet home without much strife. Each son had a girlfriend, but seemed to somehow miss out on whatever scoring system was employed to make boyfriends acceptable to the rest of the peer group.

It was all a mystery to Dot. She could sort of understand why modern females might think getting married and staying at home to raise a family might be boring, but in her opinion, anyone who managed it successfully deserved a medal. And if you could get it *right*, well, then it was so much better than any alternative that she could conceive of.

Although Dot herself only worked as a part-time cleaner, she still loved her husband and would happily kill anyone who harmed the hair on his head – let alone the heads of her two boys. She had what she felt was a good life. She and her husband had no debt, had paid off their mortgage, and could go on holiday abroad a couple of times a year if they wanted to. Indeed, she felt it was a decent sort of success achieved through applied hard work and common sense.

Dot had time to read and understand more about the world around her than many people would give her credit for, and as both of her sons had developed careers in IT, she was as well informed about the present crisis as anyone in the town. Her eldest son, in particular, had a degree in computer science and worked for an American company writing software. The fact that he did this from a desk in his bedroom was both amazing and slightly worrying to Dot. He had only graduated a couple of years ago and was apparently very well paid, so he could no doubt afford a home of his own soon, but it seemed his current situation suited him – he still had student loans to pay off, after all. Her other son, meanwhile, worked for a local engineering firm as a CNC programmer and was equally capable of moving on if he wanted. For now, though, they contributed by paying for board and keep, and Dot and her husband enjoyed a better class of holiday. So, really, everyone was happy.

Dot arrived at Caroline's house just before noon. It was a very nice, detached property on the edge of one of the town's parks. It was surrounded by trees and shrubs and had a short drive leading to the front of the house and the double garage on the side. As Dot rang the doorbell, she thought about how she rarely saw much of either Caroline or her husband these days, as they never seemed to be at home. They were a younger couple than Dot and her husband – only a few years older than their eldest son, in fact – and they sometimes had quite a busy calendar. Caroline was also never a fan of the unannounced drop-in, always reminding Dot to text or email first. Dot would do as requested once in a while but usually found it tedious. Today, with the world in its current state, there would certainly be no pre-visit emails.

With all this in mind, it was a bit of a shock when Caroline actually answered the door. When Dot had seen her in the past, she always seemed so smart and "well turned out," as her mother would have said, with perfect makeup and hair. Today, though, was different. Dot had never seen her looking such a mess. The woman before her wore a baggy sweatsuit, no makeup, and had puffy red eyes that suggested she had been in tears for some time.

"Oh..." was all Caroline said at first, looking surprised to see Dot, before standing aside to let her in. "Good of you to come, Dot."

"Are you okay, Caroline?" asked Dot as she uneasily entered her friend's house. "If you don't mind me saying so, you look, well, *awful*. Is something wrong?"

Dot suddenly regretted her words, remembering that Caroline's husband was an airline pilot and that there had been reports on the radio – the only source of information now – of aeroplanes going missing and crashing all over the place.

"Oh, Dot, everything is wrong," wailed Caroline. "Nothing is working, my phone, my tablet, my laptop, the TV. I can't talk to anyone. I don't know where my husband is, I can't FaceTime anyone or message, or text even... How am I going to order any food?"

Dot was at least relieved that Caroline's husband might still be alive somewhere. Nonetheless, she was a bit taken aback by her friend's apparent helplessness. She considered for a moment that there was obviously a generational difference between the two. Whilst she could use a computer, she certainly wasn't married to one. Caroline, on the other hand... Well, perhaps her dependence was bordering on total.

"Let's go into the kitchen and I'll put the kettle on," said Dot warmly. "Don't worry about ordering food; none of us can buy food for now. You'll have to go down the road to the school to get something to eat if you have nothing in."

"The school?" sniffed Caroline, looking confused. "Why should I go to the *school*?"

"Okay," said Dot, sitting Caroline down at the pine table in the corner of the kitchen. "We'd better start at the beginning. And first things first. Have you heard from your husband at all?"

"No," replied Caroline, looking distracted. "I tried to reach him yesterday evening when I finally made it back from work, but my phone wouldn't work properly."

"You will have to use the landline," said Dot.

"We don't have one," answered Caroline, shrugging.

"But you *do*," said Dot, looking confused. "You have that phone in the hallway; the fancy French looking thing."

"It's just an ornament," said Caroline. "I liked the shape and colours."

"Well, I've taken a careful look at the thing before, and I think you'll find that wrapped up underneath the base is a cable and socket; all you need to do is plug it in."

"Plug it in?" asked Caroline. "*Where?*"

"Oh, come on," said Dot, bridging on irritation, but trying to keep a relaxing tone. "Let's sort this out first, then. We can have a brew after."

Dot went out into the hallway and began examining the phone, locating the cable. Then, she set off looking for a socket, which she found occupied by a now redundant Wi-Fi hub. She plugged the phone in and was pleased to hear a dial tone, so she tried ringing her own number. Her eldest answered, so she explained to him the situation and asked him to read aloud the number on their telephone screen whilst she jotted it down.

"There you are, Caroline," she said, entering the kitchen once more and passing her friend a little piece of paper. "*That's* your landline number. Now, do you have a number you can ring to ask about your husband?"

Caroline looked like a deer in headlights for a moment. She was about to say all her numbers were in her phone and it wasn't working, but she suddenly recalled that her husband had a small book that he kept all his passwords in, and he had said to her once that it had some emergency numbers in the front. The book was in their home office, so the two women made their way in and began rummaging around in his desk until they found it. On the front page was indeed a list of emergency numbers for the airline Caroline's husband worked for. So, with some help from Dot, she rang it.

Some time later, she joined Dot back in the kitchen and sat down to a cup of tea and some biscuits.

"He's okay, Dot," she said, smiling with tears in her eyes. "Just stuck in Helsinki is all. I have asked them to pass on the number you gave me so he can ring me. Thank you so much, Dot. I'd have never thought of doing that. I'm truly amazed that that antique phone *works*. I feel a bit of a fool, really. I've just been in a state of panic since all my media sources packed up, and I, well… I feel a bit helpless, really."

"You are not the only one, Love," said Dot, reaching across the table and holding her hand. "But you will be okay when the shock wears off. You've only lost a phone, not an arm or a leg. Get that tea down you and have a biscuit, and maybe get changed, and I will take you down to the school. That's your local food centre, understand? You can go and get one square meal a day and some simple rations, like bread, milk, butter, and eggs. You can do that like the rest of us until they figure out what to do about the money."

"What's up with the money?" asked Caroline, perplexed once more. "I have some cash if that's the problem…"

"You hang on to your cash for now, Love," said Dot. "You won't be needing it just now. The problem, as I understand it, is that everyone's bank account has been lost. Apparently *forever*."

"Lost?" Caroline repeated. "What do you mean by 'lost'? Surely, they will be able to retrieve everything eventually, right?"

"Apparently not," replied Dot gravely. "My son tells me we have been hit by something called the 'Algorithm Plague.' I don't understand the details, but all the software has been destroyed. Meaning all the records and databases are gone and can't be retrieved." She took a sip of her tea and sighed. "See, apart from what cash there is floating about, there's simply no money. All the money that existed as computer balances has gone, and banks don't exist anymore. So, basically, no one can get paid and no one can buy anything."

Dot was quite proud of herself. She had heard all of this Algorithm Plague business and had discussed it with her husband and sons, but this was the first time she had to explain it to anyone. She was wondering where Caroline had been for the last 48 hours.

"But don't they, you know, 'back up' everyone's details every day and store them on a disc or something?" asked Caroline, incredulous.

"I asked that as well," said Dot sadly. "But my sons say it doesn't make any difference even if they have, because they won't have any means of accessing the files. Apparently, you need a computer to do that, and there aren't any that haven't been contaminated."

"And your sons are experts, are they?" asked Caroline rather sarcastically.

"Well, that could be argued," Dot chuckled uneasily. "The eldest has a PhD in computer science from Manchester University."

Caroline looked quite shocked in response to that, and Dot had to suppress not just a smile but a big grin. *Yes, madam*, she thought. *Put that in your pipe and smoke it.* But then Dot saw the defeated look on Caroline's face and felt a bit guilty. It was a lot to take in, after all.

"So, what's going to happen now?" asked Caroline after a moment of silence.

"Lord only knows," said Dot, now nibbling on a biscuit. "For now, we seem to be on a sort of war footing. Nobody's going to work other than transport workers, doctors, nurses, and the rest of the emergency services. Oh, and the army. They've managed to keep some power stations working, as apparently that was a high priority. Meanwhile, food is rationed via the feeding stations, so again, when you're ready, I'll take you down to the school and you can register with them."

"Right, thanks, Dot, really," replied Caroline, taking another long sip of tea. "But wait, what sort of food are they serving? I'm a vegan. Will they have vegan options?"

Dot sighed. "Well, it's usually meat and two veg in one form or another," she said. "But I'm sure they won't mind if you don't want the meat. If you need any vitamin supplements, you'll be struggling, so you might have to give in and bend the rules a bit for the good of your health. You needn't worry about your figure, though. Nobody is going to get fat on what we're being given, I'd wager."

Dot had meant to say this as a light joke but was horrified to see Caroline burst into tears yet again. It took her some time to calm her down, and Dot managed to distract her somewhat by suggesting she ring her mother now that the phone was working, to make sure the elderly woman was alright.

"Oh, that's a good idea, yes," sniffed Caroline, clearing the table.

"Yeah, you go and have a good chat with her, Love. I'll go and sit in the garden and wait for you, okay? It's a lovely day and would be a shame to waste it."

It was a rather stunning garden, and it was indeed a lovely day to sit in it. That said, it looked a tad overgrown just now. A friend of Caroline's usually looked after it – he had his own gardening business. A lack of fuel for his small van meant he'd be stuck at home for the foreseeable future, though, and likely wouldn't be able to cut the grass anytime soon. *The garden probably won't look this prim and proper again for ages*, Dot thought to herself.

So, she opted to take a peek in the garage and was pleased to see an electric lawnmower in one corner. Dot smiled, deciding that one of her sons could come round and cut the grass every so often. Meanwhile, she began deadheading some of the roses and pulling up a few weeds. Dot never was great at sitting still.

After a while, Caroline came out to join her, looking slightly calmer, but still a bit of a mess.

"How is your mum?" asked Dot, as the pair sat down on some patio furniture.

"Oh, she's okay," responded Caroline almost resentfully. "She almost seems to be enjoying this, to tell you the truth. She says she likes going out for her meal every day, as she gets to meet people and have a chat."

"Well," said Dot, "it's an ill wind that blows no one any good. I suppose if you're on your own, it must be nice to get out and socialise. Speaking of which, why don't you go and freshen up a bit, and we can go down to the school?"

"Alright," said Caroline, looking defeated again. "If I must, I must… But Dot, I just… I don't understand all this. What about my Facebook profile and all my contacts on my phone? How do I get them *back*?"

"You're not the only one asking, Caroline," replied Dot. "My son says things may never return to exactly what they were. If this happened because the internet existed, and if it's set up again, they'll have to recreate it in a way that stops this from ever happening again. Really, it's anyone's guess what the 'new internet' will be, and if we'll ever have open access again. If it's any comfort, the internet didn't exist in my youth, and I still had a good time."

Caroline had nothing to say in response to that. Her shoulders dropped, and she slouched off to have a shower and get changed.

Like a dog with its tail between its legs, thought Dot a little unkindly.

Dot busied herself by tidying up a bit whilst waiting for Caroline again, who reappeared looking a bit fresher and smarter. Just as they were about to leave the house, however, the telephone rang. Caroline jumped; she had never heard the thing work before, and hesitated before she picked it up, it was her husband. He was safe and well in Finland, having been grounded at Helsinki Airport. There was a group of them from the UK stuck there, and they were looking at ways to get home, either overland by train or possibly by ship, but that was more complicated, as lots of ships had to be modified in order to sail without the usual computer controls and GPS guidance. He had even heard there was a sort of flotilla of small craft sailing back and forth between

Calais and Dover, a bit like Dunkirk. However, he wasn't sure about that yet, and told Caroline he would let her know his plans as soon as he could.

After the call, Caroline seemed much more energised, and the two women set off for the school.

"He said he was lucky, Dot," Caroline exclaimed as they walked down the street. "He said that not all the aircraft had returned safely. I thought they had all these backup systems to keep them safe, but…?"

"Well, don't ask me to explain it," laughed Dot. "What I know about aircraft and two pence wouldn't pay your bus fare home. I suppose they use lots of computers to fly these modern jets, and it wouldn't matter how many backups they had. This 'Plague,' as they call it, would wipe them out in the blink of an eye from what I've heard."

They walked on in a contemplative silence for a while and shortly arrived at the school. Dot knew Margery, the lady who ran the kitchen, and introduced her to Caroline. "She lives just around the corner," Dot told her, smiling. "She's just heard from her husband, who's an airline pilot."

"Blimey," gasped Margery. "You must be relieved. They say London's in a terrible mess with all those planes crashing."

"What planes?" asked Caroline, wide-eyed.

"Haven't you heard?" said Margery. "They were dropping like flies along that route into Heathrow, like the flipping Blitz all over again."

Dot looked over at Caroline anxiously, but if anything, the news seemed to make her young friend just that much more grateful for her husband. It was clear she was having to absorb a great deal of difficult information that day, but the fact that her husband was alive and well seemed to make all the difference in the world.

"Caroline's a vegetarian," said Dot, changing the subject, and was relieved to see that Caroline didn't try to correct her.

"Then she has come on the right day," smiled Margery. "We have a very nice vegetable soup into which I have thrown a bit of pasta and called it minestrone. And we have some fresh bread rolls, too. Do you want a drop, Dot? There will be plenty to go around."

"That would be very nice, but only if you're sure you can spare it," responded Dot politely.

Moments later, Dot and Caroline sat down to a large bowl each of surprisingly delicious soup and bread. Dot had to hand it to Margery, the woman could cook – even in a crisis.

After the two friends had finished their meals, it was time for Dot to get back home to her family. She promised Caroline she'd come back to her house again tomorrow afternoon with her son so he could cut the grass, to which Caroline was extremely thankful.

When Dot and her son arrived, there was quite a commotion outside Caroline's house. Dot was amazed to see a horse and cart parked out front. It was quite a large four-wheel flatbed cart with a bench seat at the front, and in the staves, there stood a large dark bay with feathers and large feet. A big shire horse.

This sight stopped the two in their tracks. For Dot, it set off a whole series of childhood memories – she recalled the milkman's horse that used to pull his two-wheeled cart up and down the street. The horse knew the milk round as well as the milkman and would walk up the road without having to be told. She also recalled the carriage horses on the front at Blackpool – how they used to line up, and you could pay to ride them along the Golden Mile. The memory enveloped her for a few potent moments, until her son suggested they go ring Caroline's doorbell.

The sight of this horse and cart proved a great novelty for the local kids, who were soon crowded around it, wide eyed. Meanwhile, once he was done mowing, Dot's son, the PhD, emerged with a rucksack and was closely followed by an old man. Dot recognised him immediately – it was Mr. Chew, who lived by himself on a farm on the moors. He had a stable yard that he rented out mainly to young girls from the area who had ponies they kept there, and Dot supposed that this great shaggy beast must be his.

"Hello, Mr. Chew!" she called out. "That's a lovely horse what is he called?"

"Big Tom" replied Mr. Chew with a big largely toothless smile.

"That's your name isn't?" asked Dot.

"Aye" laughed Mr. Chew "He's Big Tom and I'm little'un."

"Where are you both off to, then?" asked Dot.

"The brewery," replied her son. "They have a vat full of beer they can't sell, so they've agreed that if we can find transport to collect it, we can have it on the IOU system. So, Mr. Chew has volunteered his horse and cart, and our Tony has gone to borrow the stacker truck from work."

"Stacker truck?" echoed Dot, slightly horrified.

"Yes, they have one that runs on propane gas, and his boss doesn't need it for now; he would rather be able to get a pint at *The Queen*."

At that moment, to the accompaniment of a medium sized roar, a bright yellow stacker truck appeared round the corner, complete with a pallet containing spare propane gas bottles. Mr. Chew and Dot's son both climbed up onto the cart, and the cavalcade set off for the brewery about five miles away on the edge of town.

Dot shook her head as she watched them go. Turning back to the house, she decided to go see what Caroline was up to. Maybe her friend could use a hand with something else. A little company, at the very least, couldn't hurt.

David—Caroline's Husband

You might describe David as "bland," which was both true and deeply unfair. He was a decent person — intelligent, thoughtful, kind, and loyal. He had a sense of humour, even if he wasn't great at cracking jokes, and he didn't have a malicious bone in his body. He was one of those fortunate people who loved what he did for a living.

David came from what might be described as a lower middle-class family in Cheshire. His parents were still together, having celebrated their 25th wedding anniversary some time ago. He had an older sister whom he thought the world of. Living as he did in a middle-class ghetto with a Parent, Teacher Association that was "active," to put it mildly, and parents who were educated and valued education, he received a good education at a local comprehensive school. With vigorous, supportive, and informed parents, the school had to have a good head teacher — or that person would have been shown the door pretty promptly. Fortunately for David, it had reasonably good maths and science teachers.

While still at primary school, his dad had taken him to an air show — and something clicked. He started with "Airfix" type plastic models, progressed to balsa wood planes with rubber bands, and eventually built remote-controlled gliders and powered aircraft. He was no trouble at school because he knew exactly what he wanted: to be a pilot.

His parents had no objection to this ambition, wisely understanding that having a clear aim made a huge difference. From the start of secondary school, David understood that to achieve his goal, he had to work hard because becoming a pilot wasn't easy. He joined a gliding club and the local Air Cadets at twelve and became a dedicated, enthusiastic member — so much so that he won a scholarship and earned his private pilot's license before his driving license.

He won a place at Manchester University, where he studied aeronautical engineering and graduated with a first-class degree. That made him a prime candidate for one of the few places on a funded training package with a UK airline. Though he'd enjoyed being in the Air Cadets, he didn't want the forces lifestyle.

David met Caroline through friends who were all a bit surprised they hit it off. It was true Caroline was good-looking, but she was seen as a bit shallow and something of an airhead. His friends expected him to find someone more solid and sensible. But they fell for each other, and he saw something in her that perhaps wasn't immediately obvious: a basic honesty and decency and maybe also a vulnerability that appealed to his protective instincts. They were both fiercely loyal, so once they became a pair, nothing could separate them.

Part of the truth was that Caroline was actually a bit shy and not terribly self-confident. She was determined to get on in life and tended to overcompensate a bit, so finding David made life easier and people noticed the difference in her. For his part, being with her filled an empty part of his life that he hadn't even realised existed.

David liked women and respected them. His best friend in the world was his sister, and had he taken a test of his feminist credentials, he would have passed with flying colours. It never occurred to him to treat women as anything other than equals.

He had girlfriends at school, though not really at university studying engineering didn't offer much opportunity. Despite decades of effort, the profession still only attracted enough women to make up about 10% of the total, and besides, he was too busy.

As an airline pilot, David was unusual because of his loyalty to Caroline. He worked in an environment surrounded by attractive, generally available women, but he never strayed. He treated his colleagues in a friendly, professional way, got on well with almost all of them, but never made a move at work or outside of it. Over time, and without his knowledge, he built up quite a fan club among the female staff he worked with, and Caroline was the subject of considerable envy.

He had been in his hotel room in Helsinki, getting ready to board his next flight back to Manchester, when the news started to break: all flights had been grounded. He was told to stay put and wait for instructions.

Rumours were flying. The television was still working at this point, and stories poured in from all over the world: a massive banking crisis, computer systems crashing, planes crashing. It seemed as though the world had gone mad.

He and other pilots and cabin crew crowded into the bar and watched in stunned silence. After a few hours, a manager from the airline arrived, and they all trooped into one of the hotel's conference rooms.

What the man had to say wasn't much help. He spoke in excellent English to the crews:

"I'm sorry, everyone, but the aviation industry is now at a standstill across the world, and no one has any idea when it might start up again. The information we're getting is that all the banks worldwide are dead. Their computer systems have been wiped out as indeed have ours along with all the air traffic control systems. It seems it won't be long before GPS and satellite communications are gone.

Everything we rely on to run an airline is dead. Even if our customers could access money which they can't, they wouldn't be able to purchase a ticket or check in. And if they could, we couldn't buy any fuel or fly them anywhere, even if anyone wanted to get on an aeroplane, which at the moment seems unlikely.

Please don't ask me how long it will be before things are back up and running — I don't know. But the damage is so serious and so extensive, I can only assume years, not months."

He paused to let this sink in, then continued.

"We're being advised to wait 24 to 48 hours to hear what governments across the world will do. This hotel has agreed to let you all stay for now, even though we have no way of paying for you. Obviously, there are millions of displaced people across the planet, and one urgent task will be to find ways for them to get home. Stay here for now, and as soon as we understand how to do that, we'll let you know."

Everyone trooped back to the bar, trying to absorb the news. The group consisted of twelve individuals seven men and five women. Three of the men and one of the women were pilots; the rest were cabin crew.

Dave was unusually the only Brit; the others were all Scandinavians of one sort or another. Dave sat with his friend Olaf, a Norwegian pilot.

"Bummer," said Olaf, propping himself up on a bar stool — easy enough for his long, thin six-foot frame. "I really liked this job. What the hell am I going to do with myself now?"

"Do you think that's it, then, Olaf, not just a temporary glitch?" asked Dave.

"No, I figure that's the end for me. It'll take years to recover from this, and I bet it never recovers completely. You need money flowing freely to run commercial airlines — and lots of computing power to process tickets, baggage, cargo. Not to mention air traffic control and the weather. How are we going to forecast the weather without computers?

There are probably lots of planes still okay to fly, but the general public are going to need convincing even if they had any money to buy a ticket. And how are you going to do that? Just turn up and see if a flight's available?"

They fell silent for a moment. The bartender asked if they wanted a drink.

"How do we pay?" asked Olaf.

"As far as I know, you still have a tab," said the bartender.

So Olaf ordered a large vodka, and Dave had a large whisky.

"I've no doubt in time there'll be some flights," Olaf continued. "But it'll take years to get the volume back. And there might be resistance to allowing it."

"Resistance?" Dave queried.

"Until we come up with carbon free flight," Olaf explained. "We're seen as a huge polluter. The one good thing from all this is that CO2 emissions will be drastically reduced for a while. Maybe the earth shouldn't be in too much of a hurry to build them up again."

"Well," said Dave, "it's an ill wind that blows no one any good."

He and Olaf toasted the sentiment several times with several additions to the tab, then retired to bed.

He found himself in a hotel room on the edge of Helsinki Airport, alone, with his career apparently at an end. It was as though he had hit a brick wall. All that work, all that success, a job he loved and now, nothing.

He had never suffered depression. Truth be told, he had never suffered much sadness. So, this was what it felt like when life turned shitty. His desperation was beginning to grow. The developing feeling of helplessness and frustration might have overwhelmed him.

What saved him was the telephone ringing.

It was Caroline, with a breathless and tearful story about Dot and that silly telephone she'd bought as an ornament for the hallway at home. When Caroline calmed down and they'd talked for a while, his mood lifted.

Because now he knew what he had to do. He had to get back home to Caroline. She needed him — and he needed her. They would face what was to come together, one way or another.

He couldn't dwell on it too much. A future without his beloved flying was just too bleak to contemplate. But he had always been used to having a focus in his life, and for now, he could apply that to the none-too-simple task of getting home.

David's Trip

Of all the airline staff in Helsinki at the time, David was the furthest from home — and the only one who had to cross water to get there. Forming a plan had been entrusted to Agneta, who worked in the personnel department at the main office.

Agneta was just 22 years old, from a large extended Sami family. Of average height, stocky but fit and active, with blue eyes and blonde hair, she was part of the fan club David was so blissfully unaware of. She set about the task with her usual energy, intelligence, and common sense mixed with half a wish that she could go with him.

She recruited her aunt, who worked in a charity shop, and as many friends and family as she could rope in. All David knew was that someone was working on getting him home. He was more than a little overwhelmed when Agneta turned up at his hotel a couple of days later, carrying a large rucksack and a big carrier bag.

They met in the hotel foyer. A somewhat breathless and tongue-tied Agneta took him through everything she'd put together for his trip.

"From what I can understand," she said in excellent English, "all European countries are allowing free public transport. They're keeping the buses, trains, and trams running — but how and when you catch a train is unclear. I think you just turn up and figure it out as you go. And everywhere seems to have set up feeding centres, so you should be able to find something to eat. I'm sorry I can't be more precise than that."

"That's OK, Agneta. I wasn't expecting a set of tickets and an itinerary," said David. "Where do you think I should start from?"

Agneta sat up straight and grinned.

"That's the good bit," she said. "I've got you a flight to Stockholm."

"A flight?" said David, astonished. "I thought everything was grounded."

"Yes well, all commercial passenger traffic is," said Agneta. "But my uncle Jon has a small business flying light aircraft. He has a twin-engine plane he uses for small cargo runs when he isn't taking up skydivers. The water company wants a part picked up from Stockholm pretty urgently, so my dad asked if he could do it."

"Your dad?" said David.

"Yes," said Agneta. "He works for the water company here in Helsinki. As it happens, my uncle Jon has one of his pilots stuck in Stockholm. So if you go out as his copilot, he can bring the other guy back."

"Oh. OK," said David, bemused by all the family connections. "I won't be qualified to fly his plane if anyone asks."

"Don't worry about that," said Agneta. "No one will. And Uncle Jon will give you a quick lesson when you get there. I told him you're a brilliant pilot."

She blushed and started fiddling with the carrier bag.

"Well, er, thanks, Agneta," stuttered David. "That's truly amazing and very kind of you. When is he going?"

"Oh, tomorrow," said Agneta. "So I've brought everything I could get together for the trip."

She pulled out khaki cargo pants, a checked shirt, and a bright red Helly Hansen waterproof jacket. From the bottom of the bag came a pair of almost-new hiking boots and some thick hiking socks.

"OK," she said. "I'm worried the boots might not fit. I tried to size them to go with the socks. Just try them on, and let's see."

David did as requested and found the combination perfectly comfortable.

"That's a relief," said Agneta. "You can change into the other stuff later. I've packed the rucksack with lots of things you may need — more clothes, waterproof trousers, a cover for the rucksack, a wind-up torch, and a wind-up radio."

"A wind-up radio?" said David, raising an eyebrow.

"Yes. It was my brother's, but he said he didn't want it anymore. You may need it to keep up with what's happening. The BBC World Service seems to be running OK, so you should be able to tune in, I think."

"That's brilliant, Agneta. Please thank your brother for me," said David, beginning to realise just how much trouble this young woman had gone to on his behalf.

"There's a small lightweight sleeping bag, a waterproof ground sheet, a first aid kit, some all-weather matches, packets of dried food, a Billy can, and a flask. Some energy bars for emergencies, some tea and coffee, a book of road maps of Europe, a notepad and pen, and a couple of phrase books. I managed to find Swedish, Danish, and German, but lots of people speak English anyway. Oh, and some water purification tablets, my dad says you may need them before you get back. He thinks they may run out of chemicals to treat the water."

She grinned.

"Oh, and best of all is outside. Come and look."

Agneta jumped up and led a mesmerised David out of the front door of the hotel. Leaning against the wall was a large black sit-up and beg bicycle, complete with black chain guard, rear pannier, and front and rear lamps.

"It's very old, but very well maintained," said Agneta, proud of the monstrosity. "It was my grandfather's bike. He always looked after it. It's been in my grandmother's garden shed for a long time, so everyone agreed you should have it. It's Dutch no gears, no brakes, you just backpedal. But it's all we could get for you. Bikes are suddenly very valuable now. Even with this one, I think you'll need the security chain. Here's the key."

A speechless David took the key to the bike's padlock and chain, then stepped forward to take a closer look.

"It's a Gazelle," he said.

"Yes!" beamed Agneta. "That's right. You can still get them, I think. From what I can make out, you should be able to take it on the trains. You'll need it to move around at each stop it may not be possible to keep going continuously. You might have long waits between trains."

David was taken back to his childhood for a moment and just stared at the bike. His parents had a long-standing love affair with Holland for reasons he'd never bothered to investigate, and they'd had several holidays there as he grew up. He remembered the incredulity of his friends when he said he was going to Holland, not Spain, Greece, or Disneyland. But those holidays had always been fun and always involved hiring bikes and riding on Holland's wonderful cycle lanes and tracks. He knew what a Gazelle bike was and how to ride one.

"I don't know what to say to adequately thank you, Agneta," said David. "Will it fit on the aeroplane tomorrow?"

"Oh yes, that's OK," said Agneta. "Uncle Jon said you might have to take the front wheel off, but otherwise you'll be fine. There's a spanner and a puncture repair kit in this little bag at the back of the saddle — and a pump, of course. Though you might want to look after that; it could get stolen."

"That's totally amazing," said David.

Agneta beamed at him.

"That just leaves your route," she said. "Let's go back in and look at the map. You need to head for Malmö and then cross the bridge to Denmark. Oh, and I've put my home address on these," she added, handing David a small package. "They're postcards. I thought you could let us know what progress you're making. If you get stuck anywhere, maybe we can help, you might not always be able to phone."

This was a bit of a white lie; his fan club had come up with the idea to keep track of him. But David didn't know that, and the gesture left him speechless for a moment.

"Of course, Agneta, thanks," he finally managed to blurt out. "I promise I'll send you a card as often as I can."

She rewarded him with a big, beaming smile, and they went back into the hotel to look at where he had to go.

David set off early the next morning, complete with a water bottle and some sandwiches the hotel had been kind enough to give him. He managed to strap his rucksack onto the back of the bike with some difficulty and wobbled off down the road toward the airport.

As they'd been staying in an airport hotel, he didn't have far to go, but he had to find the side entrance that would take him to Uncle Jon's light aircraft hangar, so in the end he cycled a few miles. By the time he arrived, he felt steadier on the bike and more comfortable.

They were expecting him at the security gate but were clearly amused by a pilot turning up on an old bike. It crossed his mind that all the security guys had to worry about now was theft and vandalism, presumably terrorism was less of an issue. As he approached the hangar, he saw a short, stocky guy doing checks on a twin-engined Britten-Norman Islander parked on the apron. The guy waved him over.

"You must be David?" he said, shaking hands vigorously. "I recognised the bike," he laughed. "It's a bloody old antique, to be sure, but it'll get you where you want to go. Give it to me and go into the hangar over there with your rucksack so they can sort out your paperwork. They've nothing else to do at the moment, but I don't think they'll make too much of a meal of it."

Jon had short blond hair and was almost as wide as he was tall, but he exuded confidence and competence. David took an instant liking to him. He unstrapped his rucksack and did as he was told. The formalities consisted of a guy in an office in one corner of the hangar looking at his passport and wishing him a safe trip. Within an hour,

David was seated in the cockpit of the Islander next to Jon, with the bike stowed in the back.

"You're a big jet pilot then?" said Jon as they settled into their seats. "Ever flown anything this size?"

"No," said David. "I've flown twin-engined light aircraft when I was working on my pilot's license, but they were all smaller than this."

"Not a problem," said Jon. "These are nice and easy to fly. This is fairly new, it's the BN,2T, so we've got two turboprop engines and fixed undercarriage. We'll only be in the air a couple of hours, and you can have a go at the controls. We're not carrying much cargo, just some part we're swapping for something else for the waterworks. The weather's been good and holding for some time, and the guy in Stockholm I'm bringing back says it's OK there too. We should be all right."

With that, Jon completed his pre-flight checks, and they took off for Årlanda Airport. The flight was uneventful. They flew along the Finnish coast for a while, then out over the Baltic. David helped navigate using Jon's charts and took the controls for a while, enjoying flying the Britten-Norman while Jon poured himself a cup of coffee from a flask. They chatted companionably about this and that. Jon thought that once things settled down and the politicians sorted out a currency system, short hop flying would probably be the first to get going again.

"You should go and talk to the Post Office when you get home," said Jon in response to David's worries that his flying career might be over.

"The Post Office?" said David, confused.

"Ya," said Jon. "No more email, we all go back to snail mail!" He laughed. "The damn Post Office is going to need loads of aircraft and pilots. Get into air freight if you can. It'll be the first thing to restart. They won't be so worried about passengers getting killed, and you don't have to sell tickets. FedEx, TNT, that lot will be first back in business."

David thought this was pretty astute.

"GPS is shot," said Jon, "but they can set up radio beacons. The main problem will be the Met, all those big computers predicting the weather will take a while to replace. Back to the 1960s for weather forecasts! That'll limit passenger flights for a long time."

"Do you think so?" said David.

"Ya. It won't be like after WWII when flying was an exciting adventure for the wealthy to risk their necks. No commercial company will fly passengers now unless it's safe, even if they could get enough volunteers and the authorities allowed it. Not to mention the Greens."

"The Greens?" said David, confused again.

"You know, the tree huggers. Environmentalists. They won't want you big jet boys burning up the oxygen again. I don't think we'll get back to mass air transit for a hell of a long time, but I could be wrong."

David felt Jon was probably right.

After a while, they saw Åland to their right and began crossing the small islands along the Swedish coast. Arlanda Airport was some way outside Stockholm, so the approach was over open country. They saw no other aircraft. Jon explained that although there were plenty of light aircraft that could still fly, you couldn't get fuel because you couldn't pay for it. The government controlled it, and he'd been allocated a ration because they needed these parts for the waterworks.

The airfield tower was manned, and they went through normal formalities before landing and taxiing toward a hangar. A van was waiting to take the spare parts to the treatment plant. David went into the hangar to complete the simple formalities. Jon followed him in a few minutes later, pushing the bike, which again caused affectionate amusement. David began to think it would always be a bit of a curio, perhaps an ice breaker and he was proved right a short time later.

The guys in the hangar told him the train from the airport to Stockholm was still running, though not as often. They were using it to move useful supplies stored at the airport and to support the team mothballing it. David was given clear directions and set off. He had to ride a mile or two around the perimeter to reach the station, and the entrance and platforms were pretty empty. One older man in a grey uniform and cap came over and, of course, stood back a step to look at the bike. He said something in Swedish and pointed at it. David shrugged and explained he was English.

"Ah! English," said the old man, much to David's relief. "You trying to get home on that bloody old thing?"

"Only if I can put it on a train," David replied.

"No problem," said the old man. "There'll be plenty of room, and when you get to Stockholm, you can register."

"Register?" David asked.

"Yeah," said the old man. "There was a lady setting up a desk at the station this morning, in the ticket office. She's there to register refugees like you."

"I'm a refugee?" David said, surprised.

"Yeah, I'd say so," the old man replied, gesturing at the bike. "And I think that damn thing proves it, don't you?" He laughed at his own joke, then coughed for a bit.

When he'd calmed down and wiped his eyes, he was very helpful, showing David where to wait and helping him load the bike onto a rather nice modern train.

"You're kinda lucky," the old man said.

"How so?" asked David.

"This is normally a damned expensive train ride. Now you travel for free." He shook David's hand and wished him a safe trip home. A little while later, they left the airport and set off on the 44-kilometre trip to Stockholm. David sat back and thought about being a refugee. Presumably, it would be a help. He knew that after WWII the refugee problem had been immense, and that the new United Nations had set up organisations to help. But that was about as far as his knowledge went; he couldn't remember what the organisation was called and ruefully thought he couldn't look it up on his mobile phone anymore. In fact, he was about to come under the wing of the UNHCR—the United Nations High Commission for Refugees.

The train wasn't empty, and he noticed a few small differences: the passengers were gazing out of the windows rather than staring at mobile phones, and there wasn't a headset or earphone in sight. The trip was smooth, comfortable, and uneventful. He retrieved his bike and wheeled it onto the concourse of Stockholm Central Station. As he gazed around the big open space, he spotted a desk with a blue and white UNHCR banner mounted above it. There was a lady filling in forms and a small queue. He pushed his bike over and joined it. A slight man, who looked like he might be Indian, turned and said a quiet hello, glancing at the bike.

David said hello and stood there patiently.

"You are going to Holland?" asked the Indian man.

So far, thought David, I haven't needed these phrasebooks. He guessed why the man thought he was Dutch.

"No, England," David replied

"Oh, me too. I'm trying to get to my uncle's house in Leicester. I think that'll be better for now than trying to get home to India."

"Yes, I can see that," said David. "Will you need a visa?"

"I don't know," his new friend said. "I'm hoping I can get there by claiming refugee status."

"Oh, well—good luck," David said, wondering how long that would take to sort out.

He needn't have worried. The Swedish lady at the desk was both efficient and seemingly generous. Her brief was to get every misplaced person to a place of safety as soon as possible. For her, a safe haven in the UK for an Indian refugee made perfect sense. Under the present emergency, countries were accommodating anyone who had a home to go to. When it came to David, she took his details, asked if he needed to let anyone know where he was, and gave him a card identifying him as a refugee. She understood his next stop was Malmö and explained it was an eight-hour train ride, with the next available train in the morning.

"I see you have your own transport," she said, glancing at the bike resting on its stand beside the desk.

"Er, yes—sort of," said David.

"Good," she said. "We can put you up at the YMCA on Gamla Stan for the night. They don't have much accommodation, but they'll take a few people. You can get food, a shower, and a night's sleep, then come back tomorrow morning." She proceeded to explain where he needed to go.

"It's the old part of Stockholm," she said, "with lots of narrow streets and cobbles—not so good for your bike. But if you go this way, you'll be okay." She marked out a route on a tourist map.

It didn't seem very far, so David pushed his bike out of the station.

Outside the entrance, he paused to get his bearings and suddenly felt alone and more than a little lost. He realised he was tired, and it wasn't surprising he felt all at sea. But he told himself to buck up: all he had to do was enjoy a quiet bike ride through Stockholm, and he'd feel better after some food and rest. Everything seemed in high focus a sort of heightened awareness and he felt lightheaded. He breathed in through his nose, out through his mouth, and told himself to calm down. After a few minutes, he felt better. He set off along a cycle lane on a wide, quiet boulevard, lined with tall, plain but smart buildings. After a few hundred yards, he turned right at a junction, still with the station on his right, and headed towards the water.

He crossed a picturesque bridge onto Gamla Stan island, turned left towards the Royal Palace the Kungliga Slottet and made his way onto Skeppsbron, with the water on his left. After a while, he reached the imposing frontage of the YMCA. He felt much better after the ride; the exercise had done him good. The traffic had been light: just the occasional delivery van or a few cars. Being something of a petrol head, David noticed they were all either electric or plug-in hybrids. He found out later there was a voluntary scheme to help people to and from hospital appointments, with charging points available. He propped his bike outside, unloaded his rucksack, and went inside.

He propped his bike up outside unloaded his rucksack and went into reception and offered up his refugee card to the tall thin blond guy at the desk.

"Ooh Kay you stay one night only?" the guy said in good English with a sing song accent.

"Yes, I have to catch the train to Malmo tomorrow morning" replied David.

"No problem" said the guy reassuringly "I will show you to your room, we have just finished renovating our accommodation so you are lucky, there is a café on the ground floor through that door if you drop of your bag and come down you can get something to eat and if you tell them you are catching the train tomorrow they will make you something to take with you for the journey."

"That's very kind" said David, he thought that was a bit inadequate but couldn't think of anything else to say.

"Ooh it is not a problem" said the guy "we all need to help each other and this is a Christian organisation." David suddenly remembered the bike and asked if there was somewhere to put it.

"Oh sure" said the guy and they went outside to take the back around the back of the building.

"That is a fine old bike" said the guy "How far have you come on that?" David laughed.

"Well not very far really it has been more a piece of luggage than a form of transport so far, but it brought me here from the station."

"The guy looked a bit puzzled but said nothing else and took David to his room. It had bunk-beds but David was on his own, it was clean and neat and had an en-suite shower and toilet, which surprised him, he had thought it would be a washroom at the end of a corridor, he guessed this was the refurbishment but didn't like to ask. The guy gave him a key and left him to unpack. David lay on the bunk for a moment to rest and fell fast asleep. He woke up half an hour later with a start and took a moment to remember where he was. He realised he was hungry and after washing his face he set off to find the canteen. It was a pleasant evening outside so the canteen was largely empty, David noticed a couple sat at a table together and he picked up a tray and headed for the counter, he was served a dish of what turned out to be quite good fish stew with a chunk of bread and a glass of milk. As he turned round and paused to make up his mind where to sit the guy sat with the woman waved him over.

"Whey aye man are you English, come and join us" he called out in a fairly distinct Geordie accent. David carried his tray over and said hello. The guy was clearly a big bloke in his late forties with a bald head, but he had a friendly and intelligent face, the woman seemed to be of a similar age plump with short black hair but also a confident and friendly air about her.

"You eat your stew while it's hot" she said, "Don't let Joe interrogate you". Joe gave a sharp bark of a laugh at this.

"Annie here is a southerner, so she isn't used to finding out a person's life history up front as we do up north" said Joe, "She calls that my interrogation."

"Well, I live in Lancashire" said David "so I know what you mean, we northerners are known to be friendly but half the time we are just nosey". They all grinned at this.

"It's pretty good fish stew that" said Joe "I enjoyed mine earlier" David nodded with his mouth full. While he finished Joe explained that he and Annie had both been in Sweden on business but they had been out in the sticks, they had both headed into Stockholm hoping to get home and ended up in the YMCA as refugees.

"Are you catching the train to Malmo tomorrow?" asked David between mouthfuls thinking it might be good to have some companions. Joe gave Annie a questioning look and Annie nodded.

"We think we might be better to stay here for a bit" said Joe, "Turns out we are both diabetic, we are OK here we can get what we need but we are not sure how long it will take to get home and we don't feel we can go and ask for a couple of weeks' worth of insulin, so we thought we would stay put for a bit and try and find out how difficult or easy it is to get back. Are you setting off out tomorrow?"

"Yes" said David "I have been told to turn up early for the train to Malmo, its eight hours apparently."

"Well maybe you can do us a favour?" said Joe "maybe you can write to us on your journey and tell us what it's like?" David laughed.

"No problem" he said, "I am already supposed to send post cards back to the young lady who kitted me out for the trip to let her know how I am getting on." Joe raised an eyebrow and gave David a knowing look. "No, it's nothing like that" said David "It's a long story, but she gave me some postcards with the address written on them, apparently the postal service is free as well as everything else."

"That's a good idea" said Joe "I wonder if we can get hold of some ourselves?" and he got up and headed to reception. Annie smiled at David who carried on eating his stew. He was mopping up the last remnants with his bread when Joe came back with a small stack of cards showing views of Gamla Stan.

"Olaf came through" he said "He has pointed out that if we stay in Stockholm for a while they will probably move us to a hotel as this is supposed to be transit accommodation rather than long stay, but he will be able to pass on the cards or any other mail so if we put this address on them it will be OK." They wrote the address of the YMCA on the cards and David took them to add to Agneta's, reminding himself that he should let her know he had got this far. Joe and Annie were going to walk back up to the Palace to look at the market they had heard was beginning to be set up there and listen to the buskers.

"Some of the local shop keepers have set up stalls for people to barter stuff, we don't have anything we can take but the local buskers get together to keep their hand in and they get proper audiences rather than people ignoring them most of the time, it's quite a nice atmosphere though you do get the occasional argument between people bartering." David said it sounded good but he was pretty tired, needed a shower and had to get up early to make it to the train so he wished them good luck and promised to put his home address on the last card he sent so they could let him know how they faired. He went to talk to the guy at the food counter who told him to come back in half an hour or so and he would make him a packed lunch for tomorrow. He went to his room wrote a card to Agneta, dropped it off with Olaf, picked up his lunch, went back to his room, showered and slept like a log until the clock radio in his room woke him up.

He went down to the canteen after freshening up and had a glass of milk from a dispenser, retrieved his bike and set off on a fresh cool early morning for the station. So far so good he thought it would be good if the rest of the journey was as easy as this and then he told himself off for having the thought, it was tempting fate and he had a long way to go yet. At that time in the morning the ride back to the station was even quieter with hardly any people or traffic about and the outside of the station also seemed quiet, it was a bit busier inside and, on the platform, as instructed he had arrived early so that he could load the bike onto the train. He found a guy on the platform in a uniform who showed him were to go, it seemed he wasn't the only one with a bike and they had a goods carriage specially set up to take them. He was impressed by this and relaxed a bit. He wasn't sure what he had been expecting but he realised he had been worrying about where he would put the damn thing. Even though it would be some time before the train left, they were allowing people aboard so he found a seat and stored his bag and settled down, he had a window seat with just one aisle seat beside him so he hoped who ever sat there would be OK otherwise it would be a long eight hours. But he need not have worried, it seemed that the main exodus had already happened during the time he had spent in Helsinki and while the train was busy it wasn't full, so he had eight hours to himself gazing out the window, snoozing and trying to read one of the books Agneta had given him.

He walked up and down the train to use the toilet and most people seemed to be in the same state as him, he saw one guy in a slightly dishevelled business suit and wondered what his story was but the guy was fast asleep and he could hardly wake him up and ask him. He ate the rather odd cheese sandwiches the cook at the YMCA had made for him and the apple and drank water, so the trip from Stockholm to Malmo was simply boring and he had a feeling he might have to get used to boredom on this trip, interspersed with periods of anxiety, but wasn't that the norm for travellers? He gave up analysing his situation it was pointless; stay cool and go with the flow he told himself.

The train finally arrived at Malmo and David queued up with several others to retrieve his bike, as he left the platform for the station concourse, he saw signs directing "Refugees" and found he had to queue again though several tables had been set up, so the process didn't take long. He was told he could stay in a hostel for the night and was given another little map. Trains to Copenhagen were reasonably frequent so he should return about 10.00am the following morning. On his way out he saw a Red Cross desk with a guy sat reading a book and he remembered Joe and Annie, it occurred to him this guy might have some useful information for them, so he wheeled his bike over.

"Excuse me" he said, "Do you speak English?"

"Oh ya, sort of, I guess" said the guy and gave David a big grin. "What can I do for you."

David explained he was travelling home to England and he had met two other English people in Stockholm who both suffered from diabetes and were not sure if it was a good idea to try the trip because they were unsure if they could get the medication they needed during it. He told the guy about their request for him to send back information and it had occurred to him that he should try and get some advice.

"That is a good question" he said and then proceeded to stare into space for a moment as though he was looking at something that David couldn't see. "I think they should set off now rather than wait" he said "They will only find what you have found which is people like me from the Red Cross at each station and if they came to me I would see that they could get what they needed to get to the next post, ya I think if I was in Stockholm with diabetes but otherwise fit and OK I would travel now, I cannot see things getting any better than now, it is more likely they will get worse, OK?"

"Yes thanks" replied David a bit surprised to have such a firm response, "I will send them a card."

"Can you not telephone them?" the guy asked.

"I suppose I could if the hostel has a phone I could use" said David not thinking it was urgent.

"Tell me where they stay in Stockholm and their names and I will give them a call and talk to them?" said the guy.

"Oh OK" said David feeling very grateful that someone who was much better qualified than him to give advice was going to take responsibility, he realised he had been a bit worried about what he could tell them, so he gave the guy the information and left the station feeling pleased with himself because he had shed a burden. According to the instructions on his map he had to leave the station and head for a road beside a park, because it had been such an early start it was still early evening or late afternoon and a pleasant day again so people were walking about, cycling and jogging. As with Stockholm the road traffic was light. He caught a glimpse of a sculpture of a huge revolver with its barrel in a knot and vaguely remembered reading something about it in a travel magazine. He turned left at the park and rode on with it on his right and he glimpsed a big old building on the far side of it which turned out to be the Malmohus Castle, he crossed a junction and into Malmo proper. The Hostel was a blocky white building on a corner and he decided to book in, put the bike somewhere and explore on foot. He felt like a walk after being cooped up for eight hours. The Hostel was clean and white and Scandinavian, the girl at reception said David would be sharing a room with another guy and then dropped a small bomb shell by explaining that everyone had been asked to conserve water so he could wash but not shower or bath.

"Does Malmo have a problem?" he asked.

"No, she said, everywhere does, they are worried about running out of chlorine to treat the water so we have to reduce the amount we use." David remembered Agneta saying something about chemicals but he hadn't taken much notice.

"Can I wash a few small items of clothes?" he asked, thinking of his socks and underpants.

"I should think that will be all right," she said, and showed him a small room for drying things on racks above heaters.

He unpacked a bit, washed himself and his smalls, and went to see if he could get something to eat. This time it was a sort of vegetable soup and bread perhaps not as good as the fish stew, but acceptable. He rather naively asked if there were any hot drinks tea or coffee, perhaps. The guy behind the counter laughed.

"No, sorry. Everyone is hanging on to their stash of tea and coffee. We don't know when we'll see any new supplies. I think I have some chamomile tea bags that no one is interested in."

"Thanks," said David. "I quite like chamomile tea, if you can spare it."

"No problem," said the guy. "Here." He gave David a small packet. "There are some mugs and hot water over there."

David made himself a hot drink. While he would have preferred coffee, it was a pleasant change. He thought about the supplies Agneta had given him and felt a bit guilty. He also wondered when he might make use of them. He didn't really want to let anyone know he had them but had nowhere he could make a surreptitious drink. He decided to hang on to them for now and wait and see. Refreshed, he set off to walk back the way he had come on the bike and take a closer look at the park. He walked into the park through an entry point behind some buildings on a corner and followed a path with a canal or river on his right and a lake on his left. The castle lay ahead of him, and to the left of that stood a windmill. He had always found windmills appealing and headed towards it.

On his way, he saw a guy sitting on a bench a little ahead of him. With a slight jolt, he realised he recognised him it was the guy from the Red Cross stand at the station. David went up and said hello.

"Ah, English," said the guy. "David, was it?"

"Yes," said David. "Clever of you to remember I tend to forget names almost instantly."

"Well, I had to use it to talk to your friends in Stockholm, so it stuck," was the rather less than gracious reply.

"You doing some sightseeing?" he asked.

"I've been stuck in a train for eight hours, so I thought some fresh air and exercise would do me good. It's a nice place. Did you manage to advise Joe and Annie?" David asked.

The guy took a long look at David and then said, "Yes, I got through to them. And you seem a nice guy, so I'll give you the same advice I gave them: go home and go home as quickly as you can. I've been working for the Red Cross for some time now, and before that I was in the army. I've seen many displaced persons. Your trip so far has been pretty easy, and I hope the rest of it will be, but don't count on it."

He paused for a moment and gave David another firm look.

"I know you probably need a bit of a rest now, but after this, keep going. When you get to Copenhagen, don't take time out to have a look around. Don't leave the station until your next train. Don't look for hostels. Sleep on the trains. Go hungry if you must. Don't trust the other travellers and look after your belongings. You're a refugee don't become a victim. People are okay at the moment, but things are starting to get tougher. No tea, no coffee, no beer, and now we have to be careful with water. People are beginning to worry about food supplies, and they'll stop being generous soon. Get home as quick as you can. Are you heading for Holland?"

"Er, yes," said a rather shocked David.

"Good. The Netherlanders are clever, well organised, and decent people — brilliant at logistics. Head for Rotterdam, that's what I'd advise. I'd bet money they'll get you home to England from there. What time did they tell you to go to the station tomorrow?"

"Around ten o'clock," said David.

"Get there for seven-thirty," said the guy. "There are earlier trains. And then don't stop until you get to Rotterdam."

"Okay," said David. "Thanks, I will. And thank you for the advice."

"No problem," said the guy. "Just make sure you take it." And they shook hands.

David wandered off in a slight daze, heading vaguely for the windmill. But the guy had sown some seeds of paranoia, and he started to wonder about his rucksack back at the hostel. Somewhat guiltily, he turned around and headed back, giving the guy a wide berth, he didn't need to be unnerved any more than he already was. As David walked back, he started to think about what the guy had said. He hadn't argued with him because he'd been slightly shocked by it all and had just taken it at face value. But now he wondered if he should question it. Maybe the guy was just a crank. But the more he thought about it, the more it made sense. It answered, to some degree, the feeling of unease and vulnerability he felt. He was a refugee. The world was in a crisis. He was entirely dependent on the generosity of others. He did need to get home as soon as he could, and to protect what little he had on the journey.

He headed back to the hostel and checked his rucksack in his room. It seemed okay, nothing missing. He lay on his bed and had a go with the wind-up radio to see if he could find an English-speaking station. But after messing around for a quarter of an hour, he gave up, stored it back in his bag, and read for a while. His German roommate appeared, and they had a perfunctory conversation before David got into bed and went to sleep.

He followed the Red Cross guy's instructions and was up early. After another "good wash," as his grandmother would have called it, and managing to remember to retrieve his washing, he had a modest breakfast in the canteen consisting of rye bread, cheese, and milk. He filled his water flask and set off with a degree of grim determination. He arrived at the station an hour earlier than instructed and was just in time to catch a train to Copenhagen, from where his long slog began: Copenhagen Central to Kolding, Kolding to Flensburg, Flensburg to Neumünster, and Neumünster to Hamburg. He made it to Bremen before he temporarily ran out of trains as it had become too late for his next leg.

He collected his bike, which by now he was beginning to hate, and wandered out into what he'd imagined would be a modest railway station — only to be surprised by what looked like a big modern shopping mall. He eventually found the refugee desk and explained he was English, would be catching the first train to Osnabrück, and hadn't had anything to eat all day. He was directed to a soup kitchen set up for travellers at what had been a food outlet and was given the now inevitable bowl of thick soup and a piece of bread. He devoured this, along with a glass of milk. Having refused the offer of a place in a hostel, he found a quiet bench to camp out on. He had been dozing on the trains but, much to his surprise, fell fast asleep for a couple of hours and awoke with a start — and a moment of panic in case he'd had anything nicked. But his luck was holding, and it was very quiet in the station, with all the bars and shops closed.

He made himself as comfortable as he could and waited for his next train. He left for Osnabrück early in the morning, and after three more changes at Hengelo, Amersfoort, and Gouda. He finally arrived around midday at Rotterdam Central Station. The guard on the train had to wake him up, he was getting pretty tired. Stress and an underlying concern had kept him going, but when he knew he was on the last leg to Rotterdam, he relaxed a little and zonked out. Feeling now like a piece of chewed string, he collected the damned bike and set off to find a refugee point. There was a small queue, so he had a short wait before he presented himself to a guy sitting at a desk who looked at the bike before he looked at him.

"That's quite an antique you've got there," he said. "If I had any money, I might make you an offer."

"Unfortunately for both of us, it's not for sale," said David. "I was lent it by a friend in Helsinki."

"Bloody hell," said the guy. "You haven't ridden that all the way from Helsinki, have you?"

"Er, no, not quite," replied David. "Truth is, I haven't ridden it very far at all. It's been more of a burden than a help."

"Okay," said the guy. "Well, you might need it now. I take it you want to go to England?"

"Yes," said David with a sigh. "Yes, please."

"Well, you're a lucky guy. You came to the right place. But you'll have to do some serious mileage on your bike first. Why did you come to Rotterdam? Most Brits are heading for Dover."

"A guy in Malmö who worked for the Red Cross said it would be a good idea," replied David, thinking he sounded a bit wet.

"Well, he was a smart guy. He gave you good advice. We've just heard that the first North Sea ferry has made it to Europort. If you can cycle 40 km, you'll be home tomorrow."

"Forty kilometers!" said David, trying to do the calculation in his head. "Twenty-five miles?"

"Perhaps a bit less," said the guy. "But you're in Holland—it's pretty flat, and you might get lucky and catch a lift. There are a few other Brits in motorhomes and caravans on their way. You've got until about 8 p.m. to get there. Here," he said, taking a piece of A4 paper from his desk drawer. Using a marker, he wrote HULL in big black letters, then pulled out a roll of sellotape and taped the paper to David's rucksack. "If they see that, they might stop. There's a soup kitchen over there. You can leave your bike here, I won't pinch it, get something to eat, and I'll phone up and get you a berth. Give me your refugee card."

Less than thrilled at the thought of a 25-mile ride on the old bike but buoyed up by the idea that he might be in England the next day, David went for his now familiar soup and bread. When he returned, the guy had drawn him a map showing how to get to Europort.

"You'll have to ride on the motorway for a bit to get across the river. Normally, this isn't allowed, but there's so little traffic now that no one will bother about it. You can stay off the main roads for a while, but when you hit the A4, be careful. There'll be some lorries heading for the ferry. If you follow this route, it'll take you through the safe parts of town."

"Safe?" asked David.

"It's getting a bit tricky in some areas," explained the guy. "The potheads are getting desperate and looking for things to trade. Your bike's too big and old to be of interest, but you might have something they want in that rucksack. Coffee's like gold dust."

David tried not to look shocked, but the guy gave him a funny look.

"But you'll be okay at this time of day and on those roads."

"Thanks," said David. "Perhaps it has been worth lugging this thing all this way."

"Sure," said the guy. "Good luck—you'll be fine."

David set off. To begin with, he cycled along the roads of Rotterdam, along with quite a few other cyclists and the occasional car or bus. But eventually, he had to ride up a looping motorway access road and onto the A4. This was both hard work and a bit nerve-wracking, even though there was hardly any traffic. Having a lorry roar past at sixty kilometers an hour was tricky to deal with, but he ploughed on. What really put the wind up him was riding down into a tunnel to get under the river. It didn't take long to get through, but it felt like it took hours, and he had to flog up an incline to reach fresh air. He wanted to stop, but the road system was too complicated at that point. Eventually, he reached the A5, passed through a bewildering set of link roads, and found a grass verge where he could sit and rest. Exhausted and saddle sore, he wondered if he could really do this. He drank some water, ate one of the flapjack bars Agneta had given him, felt a bit better, and, worried he'd miss his chance to get home, set off again.

The soreness got worse. He tried walking for a while, but as soon as he got back on the bike, it hurt again. Feeling rotten, tired, and sore, he'd just passed another slip road and was walking, thinking about dumping the bike and most of his rucksack's contents, when he heard a horn toot. A motorhome with a GB sticker and yellow plate pulled onto the hard shoulder. The driver opened the door, stuck his head out, and shouted, "Need a lift?" For a moment, David was too stunned to reply.

"Er, yes! Yes, thank you—that would be great," he managed.

"OK!" The man hopped out. He was tall, slim, in his sixties, with horn-rimmed glasses, slacks, and a polo shirt. "We saw the sign on your back. You're on your way to the ferry?"

"Yes. It's been quite a ride so far," David said.

"Good job we stopped then. I'm Fred."

Fred shook his hand. "Go round to the passenger door, introduce yourself to my wife Amy, and she'll get you settled. I'll put your bike on the rack."

"Thanks. Do you need any help? It's a bit heavy."

"No, no. I can manage. You take your bag and get on board."

David did as he was told. Amy, small and slim, helped him in past a seat that looked more like an armchair. She passed up his rucksack and told him to sit anywhere.

Fred soon joined them.

"Really good that rack, love," he said. "Put that bike on, no trouble."

Amy winked at David. "I was just asking how far you've come."

"Er, Helsinki," David said, surprised himself.

"Helsinki!" said Amy. "Don't tell me you came all that way on your bike?"

David gave them the story so far.

"Where are you heading for back home?" asked Fred.

David told him.

Fred grinned at Amy. "We drive past there on our way home."

They chatted. David rested. They boarded the ferry, sorted the bike and paperwork, and David found himself in a basic but welcome cabin. He washed, rested, and later enjoyed a meal with Fred and Amy. The chef had done wonders with limited ingredients. The next morning, after breakfast, they made a plan for pickup post disembarkation. Fred drove cautiously to conserve fuel, discussing everything from speed limits to the fuel crisis. They shared stories, listened to the radio, and reflected quietly as they rumbled down the motorway. They were all quiet for a while as they tried to get their heads around the magnitude of it all. Eventually, they pulled over to let David retrieve his bike and say his farewells. He promised to ring them the following day, as Amy wanted to know all about his homecoming and to be sure that everything was OK. They had more or less adopted him during the last twenty-four hours.

David was still a little sore from his exertions the day before, but he didn't have far to go. The last bit was up a steep hill, so he knew he would have to get off and push. He finally approached his house and heard voices in the back garden. He leaned the bike against the garage wall and went through the back door, only to see a rather startling sight. Caroline and Dot, the cleaning lady, were sitting on chairs in the suntrap with what looked like cups of tea. Two guys, whom David recognised as Dot's sons, were digging up his lawn. There was a stunned silence for a moment. Then Caroline let out a scream, slammed down her mug, ran across what was left of the lawn, and literally threw herself at David. He just about managed to stay on his feet. All he heard was, "Oh my God, oh my God, you made it, oh my God, you're home!" as she clung to him and sobbed her heart out.

Dot very diplomatically signaled to her sons, and they quietly left them alone. Eventually, Caroline calmed down a bit. She stood back and held his face in her hands.

"You look so thin," she said. "I can't believe you're here. It's like a dream."

They sat in the garden for a while, and David explained about the guy in Malmö who told him to get a move on and head for Rotterdam, about the ship, Fred and Amy, and his refugee status. He suddenly remembered the bike and his rucksack.

"Come and have a look at my bike," said David.

"Bike?" said Caroline. "I thought you came back by train. And didn't you fly at the start?"

"Yes, I did," said David, "but the family that helped me at the start in Helsinki lent me a bike, and I brought it all the way with me. It was a nuisance most of the time, but in the end, it was a big help. It got me from the center of Rotterdam to the ferry."

They retrieved the bike, and David opened the garage door. He'd noticed that Caroline's car was parked outside. Inside, he saw several large plastic dustbins and was hit by a rather unpleasant heavy smell.

"Ah," said Caroline. "I forgot about the home brew."

"Home brew?" said David, astonished.

"Yes," said Caroline. "Apparently the water may become unsafe to drink, so this is a weak beer or something."

"What—small beer?" asked David.

"Yes, that's it," said Caroline. "I don't much fancy it myself, but I suppose you could get used to it. Dot has been teaching me to cook, and we've been planting potatoes and runner beans in the garden."

"Oh, OK," said David, trying to absorb the idea of Caroline drinking small beer and eating homegrown vegetables she'd cooked herself. But the thought definitely cheered him up a bit.

David looked at Caroline and noticed she seemed well—and different in some way. For a start, she was wearing absolutely no makeup and looked somehow more grounded than usual; at least, that was the only way he could think of describing the difference. Calmer, perhaps. She had been such a product of her generation—so plugged in and modern. The idea that she would even contemplate home brew and potato planting was a bit weird.

"Have you been OK?" he asked, realizing he hadn't had the chance to find out so far.

"Thanks to Dot, yes," said Caroline. "I was a total mess to start with. I didn't think I'd be able to survive without my phone and social media. But Dot is old-school, and she's really looked after me. The government is encouraging everyone with a garden to plant fruit and veg. 'Dig for Britain,' they're calling it."

"What, like World War Two?" asked David.

"I suppose so," said Caroline, who wasn't big on modern history. "They're asking everybody to try and grow as many basic foods as possible, and Dot has shown me what to do with them. I really enjoy cooking now. I never thought I would. I guess I've had to finish growing up."

David took her in his arms and gave her a long hug. He was home at last, and they would face whatever came next together, with their new friends. And at some point, he would take that damned bike back to Helsinki.

The Kremlin—Zero + 7 Days

The President was annoyed. In fact, he had been annoyed for some time. The problem with being the "Strong Man" president of a totally corrupt government was that you needed access to vast amounts of money to buy all the loyalty you required—at least from those close to you in power. Of course, fear and brutality helped, but the key to success was giving key people a rich lifestyle that depended entirely on you. Buying loyalty had been a basic form of government for millennia. So, Russia's president found himself in a rather difficult situation when all the money disappeared overnight, which was a major factor in his growing frustration.

Adding to his annoyance was the fact that, while his administration was ruled with an iron fist, it was nevertheless useless in the face of a crisis of this magnitude. The food had run out in Moscow within days, and looting and rioting had been widespread. So, he decided to do what any "Strong Man" would do under the circumstances: disappear. Except, of course, this was easier said than done. That annoyed him, too.

He couldn't fly safely, he was told, and now he had a girlfriend, a couple of kids, and their damned nanny to think about. He had a small number of super-loyal acolytes in the Kremlin preparing a convoy of trucks and vehicles stuffed with food, drink, and a king's ransom in valuables—but they were waiting miles outside the city. He knew if he tried to drive out, he would probably be ambushed.

When night fell, an old Mil Mi,8 helicopter landed in the Senate Square of the Kremlin. The president, his girlfriend, the twins, their nanny, and a couple of armed guards all piled in. He had arranged for the Mi,8 because he believed its mostly analogue design would spare him from worrying about the damned computer bug. It wasn't a bad idea—it took them to a small town on the outskirts of Moscow with a railway station.

Waiting on the platform was a special train: two private carriages and two guard carriages, all spotlessly clean and immaculate. The president hustled his entourage into one of the private carriages, and the train set off.

It was a very comfortable carriage, with armchairs, tables, and a bar at one end—well stocked with anything anyone might want and manned by a waiter in a white jacket. The president's lady friend was quite impressed, but her mood was quickly ruined when she tried to open the connecting door to the next carriage and the president literally snarled at her, "Leave the damned door alone and sit down."

A little shaken, she did as she was told. She had learned not to ask questions and to obey orders, so she waited until he chose to explain what was happening. He didn't like losing control of himself, but the situation was getting to him. When he had calmed down, he explained that they wouldn't be on the train long—it was a decoy. They would stop soon at a level crossing and continue by road to a place he had ready for them, somewhere they could stay in comfort and safety until things settled down.

He had prepared it all very carefully. It was better they didn't know what was in the next carriage. It was harmless and perfectly safe, but part of a scheme he needed to keep to himself. His partner, bemused, smiled and tried to look happy, asking the man in the white jacket to mix her a cocktail.

If she had managed to open the door, she would have been presented with a bizarre and unnerving sight: the next carriage contained doubles for all of them—not in exactly the same clothes, but a man who was a dead ringer for the president and a woman who looked so much like her that she would have been annoyed had she known. But she never would. When she and the president left the train, the decoys were supposed to carry on across Russia to the Black Sea, assuming they made it that far.

Nor would she ever know that other decoy sets were travelling in different directions, some by train, some by car. The president was nothing if not thorough in his plans. Meanwhile, not far outside the town, the train stopped. They all got off. The president was ushered into a black Range Rover, and the women and children into a large Winnebago, both part of a long column of vehicles It took twelve hours to get where they were going, the last five along an isolated dirt track to a cluster of buildings in a clearing in the forest. By then, it was a late summer evening, and the president, feeling pleased with himself for pulling off this escape uneventfully, climbed out of the Range Rover and stretched as he surveyed his new domain.

He never finished the gesture. He had made two fundamental mistakes, unforgivable for an old pro like him. His first mistake: forgetting the old KISS adage, Keep It Simple, Stupid. His escape plan was too complex and involved too many people. Only one person can really keep a secret. His second mistake: asking his personal guard to drive. The guard naturally opened the passenger door to let the president out. As a result, when the president stepped onto the gravel drive, the car was between him and the house rather than the other way around. The .50 caliber bullet fired from a sniper's rifle in the trees at the edge of the clearing blew his brains out. Too many enemies, too many people involved in organizing the escape, and no money, a dangerous combination at the best of times. On this occasion, it proved fatal. His partner was allowed to keep the Winnebago.

Similar things happened to all the so-called "strong men" around the world, usually followed by a takeover by the army. While military men make very poor civilian leaders in the long term, armies do tend to have a reasonable grasp of logistics. For the populations in Russia's big cities, having the army in control was their best hope of getting something to eat at least in the short term, though what happened was far from perfect, thanks to Russia's abiding disease: corruption. With the president gone, the country still had a prime minister and the Federal Assembly. So, on paper at least, they had a functioning government. It has been said of Russia that while it is never very efficient, it can be effective. The PM wasted no time in calling in the chiefs of staff, and they agreed that they could manage without a president for the time being. A new one could be sorted out later. For now, they would try to follow the same pattern as the West: keep the power and transport running and somehow set up feeding stations for the population.

They were realists. They knew this would result in theft, corruption, and a degree of mayhem, but they had no choice. Meanwhile, the PM thought to himself that perhaps he could rummage around in his metaphorical cupboard and find an olive branch to wave at Europe and America. The chiefs of staff were relieved. They had endured years of nonsense about threatening NATO. They were painfully aware that, while they had a large number of armed forces, most were poorly trained and equipped. Though they appeared to have a lot of kit, the supply chain was so corrupt that much of it was inoperable. They had been amused by reports of the German army having no spares and its soldiers being too fat, at least it sounded like the Germans had decent food. Deploying the troops to help the people might at least stop them from deserting en-masse.

The general of the Moscow garrison met with the city's mayor at his office on Tverskaya Street. The general had a healthy dislike of politicians, but he knew the mayor personally and knew he could work with him if he had to. He also knew what the mayor wanted: soldiers on the streets. After the usual meet and greet session, they got straight down to business.

"I need your men to back up my police to stop rioting and looting," demanded the mayor.

"Are you sure about that?" asked the general. "My young soldiers are barely trained to be soldiers, never mind policemen."

"They can guard things, can't they?" said the mayor, a bit petulantly.

"Yes, as long as it's painted green and looks ugly," said the general. "You're going to want them to guard shops and stores full of desirable goods. They may prove to be more efficient at looting than the general public. And you really don't want them wandering the streets with loaded guns, the public is fed up with the situation as it is."

"Exactly," said the mayor. "That's why I need them."

The general stared at him for a while and said, "OK, let's do it this way. If I can get enough of them, I'll park some tanks at strategic points around the city and man picquets to guard them. They won't actually have any ammunition, they'll just be there to intimidate people. I'll also station groups of troops in trucks at various locations and rotate them every four hours. If trouble flares up, you can use them. To be honest,

I don't have that many to spare. Most of them are moving food around and running kitchens, and you don't want to go the same way as the president or 'do a China.'"

"Do a China?" asked the mayor.

"Perhaps you haven't heard," said the general.

"Heard what?" asked the mayor, looking worried.

"Paranoia," said the general. "All so, called 'strong leaders' suffer from it. They climb their way to the top by stabbing people in the back and using the knives as rungs on the ladder. When they get up there, they suddenly feel exposed, and generally scared shitless, so they have every reason to feel paranoid.

"The Chinese solution has been to use high tech to try to keep tabs on all 1.4 billion people plus visitors. They even have facial recognition machines handing out toilet paper in public bogs, for crying out loud. CCTV on every corner. You get a text if you jaywalk too much. They've 'nudged' the population towards a cashless society so they can monitor every move anyone makes. Did you know they reward people for paying their bills promptly? Now, all that surveillance has gone totally blank. The party leaders have no idea what is happening anymore. They are suddenly blind. So what do they do? They put the Red Army onto the streets.

"But even though it's a big army, it isn't big enough, and they're spread out really thinly. They're no better trained than our lads. They've either just been giving up and going home, or they've been throwing their weight about, which has really annoyed an already disgruntled public who know they've done nothing wrong. The result? Chaos. The party has lost control of large parts of China. The Uyghurs were the first to break out, and the local Red Army are barricaded in their barracks. Most of the main Communist Party members have gone into hiding. China is a basket case.

"The moral of the story is, Mayor: try not to be too paranoid. Use your armed forces to help where you can. Do not use them to oppress your own citizens, and if you must use them in a military fashion, do it sparingly."

"OK" said the Mayor, a few tanks and troops in trucks, I get the picture." And he went to get the Vodka out of the fridge.

Russia's ancient second arm of government, the Mafia was also at something of a loss. It had plenty of cash, but that wasn't much use if there was nothing to buy and nothing had any value anymore, they could trade in sex and food and drink, which they did but it wasn't on the same scale as drugs and protection rackets. The drug supply had dwindled to a dribble and never having been great farmers trying to control agricultural output was a new enterprise. At first, they were pretty hopeless, but given time they would no doubt get a grip and become a nuisance again. The ordinary Russian people did what they were used to doing the suffered. The laws of unintended consequences took over and many strange events happened. The fact that the Russian Army saw no point in a political stand-off that had been in place for decades was a huge relief to everyone, especially to Germany who needed to keep the gas flowing but also to everyone else who wanted Russia's Nuclear Arsenal to be safe, but an odd side effect of this rapprochement was the opening up of the prospect of some air travel much sooner than had been expected. The Russians still flew old Yak and Tupolev short and medium range passenger aeroplanes that had been designed and developed when "Fly by Wire" meant steel wires not copper ones and the electronics were all analogue not digital and the algorithm plague had had no effect on them. True, they needed old fashioned pilots to fly them but Russia had those as well so the Russians started a sort of international Taxi service for Europe and eventually flew a collection of European leaders to New York via Reykjavik for a meeting of the UN council to try and work out what to do to get the world economy working again.

For Pieter and Ivan all this flying around Europe was great, with the help of NATO and some cooperation from the Red Army, a series of radar stations and radio posts had been set up so the Russian pilots could navigate easily by flying from waypoint to waypoint. Whilst coverage was not one hundred percent they were tracked for most of the time to make sure they were at least roughly where they thought they were and not miles off course. The Met was a bit of a problem however, as all the old metrological data collection and processing system was now defunct, weather forecasting was back to pre-computer days only worse because the old system for gathering data didn't exist. The army helped a bit and some sort of system was cobbled together, based on simply phoning ahead and hoping for the best. As they were (like most of the Russian pilots) ex Red Army Air Force, they were quite good at "Flying By the Seat of Their Pants" and were confident they could make the trip, over to Holland and Schipol Airport to pick up their passengers, up to Reykjavik to refuel and on to New York. They would have an overnighter in Reykjavik and several days in New York before the return trip so this was, for them, something to look forward to.

United Nations—Zero + 1 Month

For Professor John Davenport, on the other hand, who was a nervous flyer at the best of times, the trip bordered on being an absolute nightmare. What eased his anxiety somewhat was the fact that the RAF had its own equivalent of the Russian planes. Indeed, somewhat amazingly, they still had in service a couple of VC10s, known by some to be the Rolls-Royce of passenger aircraft especially in comparison to the Russian Ladas. Anyone who had had the privilege of flying a VC10 could speak to the brilliance of the engineers who had designed it and had logically assumed that putting the engines at the back of the fuselage would mean a quieter flight. Whilst this was technically true, it skipped over a point of detail regarding access, serviceability, and running costs.

And so, for Professor Davenport, it was simply a great relief to fly RAF and have a direct flight across the Atlantic. He was rather exhausted, having been working flat out since the start of the crisis, and having been thrust into the spotlight as a world expert on the "Algorithm Plague." And now, of course, he was expected to give a presentation to the UN assembly. Never an easy thing to do for the average person, surely, but made all the worse by the numerous questions sure to be asked, which he was supposed to be able to answer. He could certainly try his best, but he knew he'd feel overwhelmingly exposed as a fraud, and, what's more, would no doubt be very boring without his beloved PowerPoint.

Nonetheless, John Davenport had managed to cobble something together for himself – producing a projection from his laptop. Having worked this out, he managed to persuade the man managing the trip that his collection of hardware was essential luggage. All he had to do now was survive the flight, and so, he had developed a deep faith in the skills of the RAF. Luckily for John, he missed out on the sight of the two Russian pilots who had flown the European contingent to Reykjavik, knocking back copious quantities of hard liquor in the hotel bar and then looking hale and hearty at breakfast the following morning. The passengers who *had* observed this were of a more forgiving nature and concluded that the pilots must have the constitutions of oxen. It's safe to say that everyone aboard was relieved to step down onto the runway in New York and many were in sharp denial of the fact that very soon they would be back aboard for the return leg.

The trip through New York to their hotel was an odd one. It was a city they had all visited often and knew quite well, famous for its noise and energy and endless traffic, but not now. It wasn't deserted, of course, but the buzz was gone. People were on the streets as usual, but the traffic was a fraction of the normal amount. As John gazed around Manhattan through a bus window, he thought, *New York without money isn't really New York*.

Waking up in his hotel room the next day, John wondered what the state of the assembly would be like. Rumour had it that there would be plenty of vacant seats, especially from sub-Saharan Africa. Kleptocracies had not fared well. The total absence of money had destroyed the delicate balance that kept the leaders alive, and the settling of old scores had done little for the general population. As ever, the weak and vulnerable had suffered the most, and the men with guns had survived. No one knew quite how bad things were. The days of 24-hour news coverage worldwide were over, and so the faces of those who appeared at the UN conference would tell one tale, and those who did not another.

John knew that the message he had for those who did turn up today was not going to be an easy one to accept. It would likely be received badly by some and possibly resisted, but the days when an engineer was considered a nuisance by confusing an issue with facts were over. What he had to say to the assembly was unequivocal, and they had to understand it and accept it. Otherwise, mankind was doomed. This thought made him feel a little sick in his stomach, but he also knew that what he would present would be a series of facts. No supposition. No political dogma. And as long as he hung onto facts, it would not be his fault if the politicians did what they normally did and bugger everything up. He was reasonably confident that things would work out; he knew that everyone in the UK group was on board and that they had been working hard to prepare the ground. In truth, he didn't need to convince *everyone* – just the main players. He had been led to believe that the G9 were pretty much there in full force, and what they needed to do was add the other 11 countries of the G20. After that, everyone else would fall in line, and his role would just be to lay the foundations for an approach first invented by Margaret Thatcher: "There Is No Alternative," or "TINA" for short.

On his ride over to the UN, John Davenport had the unusual feeling of butterflies in his stomach. He had never really suffered from what one might call "stage fright"; he enjoyed lecturing and presenting papers at conferences but overall, his audiences were never all that critical. He had never had to present on such a grand stage with so much at stake. As he stepped up to the podium, he quickly decided to ignore the rest of the room and just present what he had to the UK contingent. That way, he could soak up the atmosphere only after finishing his presentation.

John started with the classic lines, "Good afternoon, ladies and gentlemen." He had already been introduced by the chairman of the gathering, and he had already set up a picture on the screen behind him. It was a section of code. Lines of words and numbers that would make very little sense to anyone other than a computer programmer, and in this particular case, it would likely make little sense to one of them, too.

"What you are looking at is a section of the Algorithm Plague, as it has come to be known," said John, speaking carefully into the microphone.

He paused then, as a slight murmur made its way through the room. John could feel the tension heightening all around him. *This* was it, after all. This was the reason they were all here, and none of them had ever seen it before, not even the UK team.

"Now," John continued, "I don't know if any of you are keen software programmers?"

He paused again briefly, allowing for a nearly inaudible chuckle from those who appreciated a bit of irony.

"But even if you are, I'd wager you'll find this bit of code difficult to read. See, if this were a piece of art, it would be up there amongst the greats. It's a Da Vinci, a Michelangelo, a Rubens. Pick your favourite amongst the masters, and that is what you are looking at here. Because in its own weird and ridiculous way, it is a work of sheer genius. If we ever find out who wrote this, we need to employ them. Not punish them."

This last statement caused a larger ripple of murmuring around the room, so again, John waited a moment.

"Look, I do not understand why it was written," he said, all humour gone from his voice. "And my team and I are only able to guess as to its purpose. But what you are looking at is not the original code. This is what it 'evolved' into, and I want to emphasise that point; that word, 'Evolve.' Why? Because it seems that this code can, in fact, do that."

The volume of the muttering from the room rose a few more decibels. John had not intended to stop at this point, but the reaction surprised him a little. He gave everyone a few more seconds to settle and then continued once more.

"We think, and I emphasise '*think*,' that it started out destroying what we would call 'legacy' software written in now defunct and unused software languages. You might be surprised to find how much of that is, or was, still out there. But it had either an extremely clever add-on ability or an error in its design, which allowed it to include other similar programming languages. What we use now are evolutions of these older programming languages, so once it had destroyed all the legacy software, it found it could move onwards and upwards to destroy pretty much everything it encountered."

Here, John had intended a short pause, and yet the room was pure silence.

"And this is an important point," John said, leaning into the microphone. "And that's because this thing's only reason for existing is to destroy software; to obliterate lines of code. There is no facility to steal or capture data; it isn't interfering temporarily so that blackmail can occur. It is designed to implacably, and with stupendous efficiency, *destroy* software. Whilst at the same time using software to essentially move around from virtual place to place. Once it infected the internet, nothing could stop it. Not firewalls, passwords, or security protocols. These are all software of one form or another, and this piece of code can travel amongst them to reach batches of code written at whatever level it has evolved to. As we've found, it seems to look for a certain bulk and then obliterate it. With that in mind, it will take us a long time to fully understand how it works. And, in fact, we may never truly understand *why*. But from the moment it was released, any computer that was switched on and connected to the internet in any way, shape, or form was dead, and will remain dead because this thing can lie dormant in areas of non-volatile memory forever. Therefore, the computers that are dead must remain so; any attempt to repair them will risk releasing this virus again. Indeed, you could say that attempting repairs will be futile." He took some time to let that sink in, as well as to take a sip from a water bottle that had been left for him on an interior shelf of the podium.

"Of course, not all devices were contaminated; any that were turned off or not connected to the internet at the time of the collapse have survived intact. As you can see, I am using a laptop to project this picture, and without any link to any other computer, it will remain perfectly functional. However, if we set up the internet again in the future, we must never allow any of the contaminated computers to be linked to it, unless in the interim we invent a completely new method to write software that even this virus will not recognise. For now, we are back to a position we were in before the internet was invented. We have computers, and we can certainly design and build more. But we must be very careful if we want to link them up again. And as for the banking computers, which I know are the priority of this conference… Well, they are gone, destroyed, and beyond recovery."

As John expected, the room burst into a cacophony of loud murmurs and comments at this point. This was not really news to anyone at this point, but many had still been hoping for some sort of miracle, which no one could supply.

When the room had settled enough, John resumed. "I know that this is difficult to accept and understand, and that people have assumed or at least hoped that it would be possible to somehow access the digital records stored in various banks' computer databases. There may be some nonvolatile memory out there that has not been wiped clean but accessing it has proven to be impossible. Believe me, we have tried. Our best estimate to date is that if we struggle with this problem as our main priority for the next year or two, we may recover one or two percent of the data that is out there. That said, it will never be possible to recover more than a percentage of the whole, which is a hopeless feat. And if we cannot resurrect all of it, we cannot reboot the banking system. A partial reboot is simply not good enough. If we could achieve 90%, maybe, but 40 or 50% just won't work. I'm afraid that we all must accept the fact that the world's banks don't exist anymore as coherent entities and that the money they had in digital form is gone forever."

John was not sure how they would react to this particular part of the presentation, and the total silence that followed was both a surprise and a little unnerving. He waited for a short while and then asked if anyone had any questions. One of the delegates asked for the record, so he could explain what he meant by "nonvolatile memory." John had anticipated this, so he changed the image to that of a circuit board with several silicon chips.

"My guess is that most of you will have used a word processor at one time or another," he said, gesturing up at the projected image. "You will know that if you don't 'save' what you type, you may lose it when you turn the computer off. This is because computers use 'volatile' and 'nonvolatile' memory. The volatile memory works whilst the computer is powered up, but data can also be stored when the computer is shut down. This, then, is nonvolatile memory. And most of the processor chips you see on this board will have some nonvolatile capacity. The thing is, this virus could lie in wait in one or all of these chips, ready to break out as soon as power is reapplied."

The delegate thanked him, and the room fell silent again. After a little while, the chairman asked the room if anyone else had any more questions, and as no one did, he thanked John, who left the podium feeling totally drained. He went to sit with the UK delegates, who all quietly thanked him and congratulated him. As John took a seat, the UK's ambassador to the UN, a very friendly and surprisingly ordinary lady, leaned into his ear. "I know we all knew what you would say in advance, John," she whispered, "but well done. It had authority and left no room for doubt. Now, we can get down to the nitty-gritty."

John nodded at her and smiled. He had not deliberately set out to put his stamp on anything, and so he had not really realised how the presentation would come across. "Authority" was a good word, he reckoned. It made him feel like he had done what he had to do, which, when he looked back on it, was quite a big ask. In effect, he had just told the whole world that banks didn't exist anymore.

John had, for a while, a ringside seat to an enormously important piece of history. If – and it was still a big "if" – the people in this room could come to a consensus about the way ahead and agree on a common set of rules, it might be possible to get the world economy going again. It wasn't going to be easy or instantaneous, but it could happen. And if it did, it would be a far, far better alternative than worldwide chaos and anarchy. The basic idea was simple: The only money left in the world was cash. And at any given time, the amount of cash in circulation in the developed countries of the world amounted to about 10% of the money circulating in the economy. It would take too long to manufacture the other 90%, so the idea was to pick a time and a date and divide the value of everything – except the cash – by 10. A car that would have cost £30,000 would now cost £3,000. A house that was worth £250,000 would now be worth £25,000. But the value of cash stayed the same, so that a £10 note would buy what a £100 note would have bought before the change. In a very simple and crude way, they were going to try and match the value of the world economy to the cash in circulation so it could move again.

Of course, this presented immense logistical problems. Each country would have to set up a national bank, and each of those countries would then have to arrange a means of injecting cash into circulation; it was the details of all this that were to be debated today, and as always, the devil was in the details. What could you do, for instance, with large denomination banknotes? A £50 note would be worth £500, which would be impractical. For the UK, the biggest denomination would have to be the £5 note, and the 1p would be worth 10p; it was clear there would have to be a smaller denomination than that. Solutions would have to be hammered out, though there would certainly be a constant background resistance from the few remaining Kleptocracies and the more corrupt governments. This is because amongst these solutions, there was one that would allow large quantities of large denomination notes to be deposited in these new national banks, provided the owner could prove the legitimacy of the origins of the ownership of the cash.

Meanwhile, drug barons and organised crime would not be welcome; an idea that would present some of the world's many corrupt politicians with sleepless nights. The other idea that caused a great deal of debate was the cash handout. The point of this idea was to try and essentially kick-start economies by giving every adult in the country a fixed amount of cash every week for a set period of time. This would be a sort of national wage that could allow people to start consuming again and manufacturers to start producing.

The question of how much money was to be given – and for how long –would rage on for quite a while until some sort of formula based on each country's average earnings could be sorted out. Indeed, it would take some time, but the result will be an inevitable one, because America, Europe, Russia, and China have already decided to take this route. As such, the rest of the world will have little option but to follow on. How it would be enacted worldwide was another story yet to be written, and no doubt, the weakest would suffer the most. That said, they would probably suffer even more if the world fell into chaos.

And so, a date was set, the conference broke up, and the delegates went home.

Zara—Zero + 6 Weeks

She just needed him to leave, to get into that horrible car of his and go wherever he went on his trips. She was ready now. She had collected all the documents she needed: the birth certificates, the V5 form for the car, and even her passport, though that worried her in case he noticed it had been moved. She had bags and toys packed in boxes, all her jewelry tucked into a bag, and her aunt and uncle were ready and waiting for her. It had been an exhausting few weeks, full of fear and creeping around, trying to do everything without him noticing, but she was sure she'd succeeded. All she needed now was the chance to run. Living in this gated community made it harder. There was only one way out, a single road. If she timed it badly and he came back as she was leaving, he'd see her, and that would be the end of it. But she had to take that risk. This plague had given her a chance, a chance to escape without him finding her.

At first, when it all started, she'd been distraught. Her only real links to the outside world had been her phone and iPad. When they died, she sat and cried for an hour, thinking she might finally lose her mind. But then, somehow, a thought crept in: without them, he wouldn't be able to keep tabs on her anymore. She was sure he did. She felt certain he always knew where she was, probably tracked her phone, fitted something to her car, and somehow knew whenever she used her credit card. But all that would be dead now, wouldn't it?

The question was, where could she go? Unless she found somewhere he'd never guess, it would be pointless. It had to be a place he didn't know, somewhere he couldn't find out about by threatening her friends or family. Family wasn't a problem, there was only her mum, who was in a care home. She didn't recognise her anymore, and he never visited, so he'd struggle to learn anything useful there. Maybe, just maybe, there was somewhere safe: Uncle Fred and Aunty Amy. They weren't actual relatives, just old friends of her father's, but she'd always called them Uncle and Aunt. That lack of a true family link might make them harder for him to trace. Her mum still got a Christmas card from them each year, and Zara had sent one back on her behalf when her mum hadn't been well enough. She had their address, and, crucially, their phone number, in her mum's address book. They didn't live far, but maybe that didn't matter, so long as he had no idea who they were.

So, she started to plan her escape. She needed him to go out after she'd picked the children up from school, keep the routine going, or leave during the weekend. But time was running out. She had to act before this next payday came so she could set up her own bank account. He was out now, but she had to wait a little longer to fetch the children. She always picked them up on foot, so she'd have to come home first. She didn't know how long he'd be gone. She was agonizing over whether to take the risk when events took over.

She heard the car arrive, and, strangely, the garage door open. He didn't usually bother putting the car away; he liked leaving it on the drive, looking sinister with its matte, black paint job. The door from the garage burst open, and he stumbled in, supporting that horrible friend of his, the one with the tattoos and the dead eyes who always looked at her like a piece of steak he was about to bite into. But now he was in pain, clutching his hand over a blood-soaked T-shirt. She was too stunned to speak, and at first, they both ignored her. The kitchen was large enough for a dining table and chairs. Glen pulled one out and dropped his friend into it.

"Quick, get a towel," he said, and Zara handed him a hand towel. He pressed it over the wound, pausing to catch his breath.

He glanced at Zara, but she had her back to him, rummaging through a cupboard. He was about to snap at her when she turned, holding a first aid kit.

"Thanks, doll, that's a good idea. What's in it?"

"Probably not enough," said Zara. "It's just plasters and a bit of bandage. There's some antiseptic. You'd be better off getting gaffer tape, maybe tape the towel in place, or use another one." The towel was already darkening with blood. "He needs a doctor. I've got to go get the kids."

She met Glen's gaze, surprised at how calm she felt, and watched emotions flicker across his face, anger, confusion, fear, before he got a grip on himself.

"I can't take him to a hospital, it's a gunshot wound. But we have a tame doctor who can patch him up. Get another towel. I'll find the tape."

So, the chance she needed fell into her lap. She fetched a clean towel while Glen grabbed the black gaffer tape. Together, they bound up the wound as best they could. While the two of them staggered back to the garage, she grabbed her coat and bag and set off to collect the children. She was a little late, but not too much. She apologised and got them home as quickly as she could. As she'd hoped, the car was gone. Moving fast, she gathered everything she'd prepared, bundled the children into the car, and ran for it. She was a competent driver, but her adrenaline was so high she was shaking. She forced herself to take deep breaths, in through the nose, out through the mouth, to steady herself.

The children, thrilled to be in the car again, were content and blessedly quiet in the back. She knew where she was going. Once she turned off the main road toward the house, she could relax a little. She was heading north; she was pretty sure Glen would be heading south, toward Liverpool.

The roads were so empty it felt like driving late at night. She felt like she stood out a mile, but she was confident she'd gotten away so far. She was sure she could handle the car, a big, black Japanese plug-in hybrid SUV. He'd given it to her for her birthday, with silly fanfare, balloons, and ribbons, just another tool of control. She'd liked her old car; she suspected he'd been given this one somehow. But that didn't matter now. He'd put her name on the registration document, she'd found it in his study, and that was important. She'd heard on the radio: people could drive if they could prove ownership. The DVLA was gone, and so were the insurance companies. The government guaranteed basic third-party insurance. People didn't drive unless they had petrol, but this, this had range. The battery alone might get her to Fred and Amy's, and if not, it had nearly a full tank. She just had to hold it together for another half hour, and she'd be safe, free from the golden prison she'd somehow ended up in.

She thought back to when she first met him outside a nightclub in Liverpool. He was a bouncer on the door, and she was with a group of friends on a night out. Had it been love at first sight or lust at first sight? Possibly love on her part and lust on his. She had been barely twenty, and it was the first time she'd gone out in a while. The previous few years had been hard for her. She had done reasonably well at school, taken her A levels, her results weren't brilliant, but she could have gone to university if she'd wanted to. But she had suffered a series of losses: first her grandparents, who she'd spent a lot of time with as a child, and then her dad, who she thought the world of. Her mum wasn't coping very well, and she felt adrift, as if nothing she used to rely on existed anymore. The thought of leaving home at that point just wasn't possible. A family friend gave her a job in her hairdressing salon, and she started training. It kept her busy, and she had an artistic streak that found a way to express itself. It wasn't what she'd planned to do, but then, she hadn't really had a plan.

She made new friends, as most of her school friends and her boyfriend had disappeared off to uni. Truth be told, that didn't bother her much. While she didn't have it in her to make a fresh break, she did need to move on, and gradually, her self-confidence returned.

Then she met Glen.

He made her go weak at the knees the first time she saw him. Looking back and knowing now how controlling he became she must have seemed like such an obvious target to him. But she had meant something to him, she was sure of that. Perhaps it was her air of innocence, her lack of baggage. She wasn't a virgin, but she was probably the nearest thing to one he'd find in Liverpool. Maybe it was that. But he concentrated on her, swept her off her feet, as the saying goes, with his flash cars that she never really liked, the parties, the holidays. It had been a lot of fun. And while her antennae had been twitching and some things hadn't seemed quite right, she was far too smitten to really bother. Then she fell pregnant, and the long road to this point in her life began. From feigned concern to total control and at the same time, her mother's health deteriorated. Whatever minor bad things Glen had been doing when she first met him had grown into a veritable criminal empire. Ostensibly, he ran a security business, but she'd realised a long time ago it was drugs. She didn't smoke, barely drank, and as far as she could tell, Glen wasn't an addict, though she'd seen him use coke occasionally. He laughed it off when she disapproved. It was so common among the young, flash set they mixed with at first that she shrugged it off. But being pregnant and effectively alone in the world left her helpless to avoid the trap he put her in. And it was a subtle trap; it took her a long time to understand how tight it was. The move into the house she'd just left was perhaps the final straw.

She had been pregnant again when he announced they were moving. She'd had no say in it. On the face of it, most people would wonder what she had to complain about: a brand new five-bedroom detached house on a small, gated plot in a desirable, leafy middle-class town north of Liverpool, close to the coast. Her mother was now in a nursing home and beyond remembering who Zara was. So why not live in this pleasant spot?

Because she knew no one. Because she was cut off from the few friends she had left. Because her neighbours had their own reasons for staying aloof. Because for her, it was more like a prison than a home.

The baby arrived, and she let herself fall into a simple, routine life for the sake of the children. But she felt watched, checked on, restrained. And it oppressed her. At first, when the plague happened, she felt like she'd become deaf and blind. Her only outlet, apart from shopping and taking the children to school, had been her mobile phone and tablet. The plague took this last link away from her, but it blinded him as well. He could no longer keep tabs on her. This plague had cut all those invisible strings he'd tied to her wrists and ankles. She had been cut free. She was off and running.

When she arrived at Fred and Amy's bungalow, she saw a motorhome parked in front and drove onto the drive. They must have been waiting at the window; they came out straight away to help her take the children and her things inside. Fred took the car keys from her so he could put it in the garage. When he'd done that, he put the motorhome back on the drive.

"How are you, love?" asked Amy, while Fred busied himself sorting the vehicles out.

"OK, I think, Aunty Amy. A bit shaky," said Zara, sitting down in Amy's kitchen.

"I was going to offer you a cup of tea. Would you like something a bit stronger? I have a nice bottle of Albariño in the fridge, we got it last time we were in northern Spain."

"Could I have both?" asked Zara. "I could murder a cup of tea, but a bit of alcohol might stop me shaking."

Amy smiled at her. "Of course you can, love. Try this and tell me if you like it," she said as she poured Zara a glass of white wine and switched the kettle on. "Do you want to talk about what happened, or would you rather just forget it?"

"Same answer," said Zara, and gave a harsh laugh. "I need to tell you, but I'd rather forget it." She took a swig of the wine and was about to start talking again when she looked at the glass and said, "This is nice. What did you say it was?"

"Spanish white, from Galicia," said Amy. "Good, isn't it?" And they both laughed.

"He came back with this creepy pal of his who'd been shot," continued Zara.

"Shot?" exclaimed Amy, looking aghast.

"Yes, shot," said Zara ruefully. "Couldn't have happened to a better person, if you ask me. But I suppose in the end he did me a favour. It was quite a bad wound, so Glen had to take him to some crooked doctor he knows, and I had to go and pick the kids up, so the timing was right. I knew I could get away before they came back."

Amy said nothing immediately. She gave Zara a hug first. "You poor thing. You're a brave girl. I'm proud of you. And don't worry, you'll be safe here. We'll look after you, and you can start afresh whenever you're ready to. There's no rush. Fred has been looking into everything we need to do to get you set up for Payday. We can go through it all with you later. Help yourself to another glass of that if you want, we have plenty."

"Thanks, Amy," said Zara. "You know I'll never be able to thank you enough for helping me like this."

"Don't give it another thought, Zara love. You're as near to family for us as makes no difference, and we're happy to help, so forget it. Having you and the little ones safe and sound is thanks enough." Amy gave Zara another hug.

Zara sat for a moment and let the tears flow. The strain she'd been under had been horrendous, and the realization that she had succeeded, that she and her children were free, clear, and safe, and that she was here with people she knew and loved, was almost too much to bear. Too much to accept. It all felt surreal. Deep down, what hurt most was knowing she would never see Glen again. And while she had grown to fear and loathe him over the years, she also knew she would miss him and that was really difficult to cope with. But cope she must and cope she would.

Glen

The doctor had been struck off for drug addiction, and Glen had found him useful, so he fed the addiction. It was a simple controlling mechanism. Glen liked to be in control; he had ever since he was a child. Had anyone ever diagnosed his mental health, they might have said he was a high, functioning sociopath, but no one ever had, and Glen wasn't interested. He was born at that time of year that meant, when he went to school, he was always the oldest and usually the biggest in his class. He wasn't especially cruel as a child, but he had no empathy for much of anything. If anyone had given him a dog, he would have been interested only in training it to do what he wanted and if that meant hurting it, it wouldn't have bothered him in the slightest. He discovered quite early on that he could select a "slave" someone who would trail around after him and do whatever he wanted. Sometimes, he could collect a few of them and have his own gang. As he grew older, his gangs became more and more threatening, though he was never actually caught doing anything that might have led to a brush with the law.

By the time he was in his teens, his parents had abandoned any hope of having any influence over him, though his dad had taken him to a local boxing gym in the hope they could teach him some self-discipline. This was a mistake on two levels: one, because Glen didn't lack self-discipline, he just applied it to things that interested him, not to what his dad thought he should and two, because he learned to become fit, strong, and dangerous. He learned something about receiving pain, but much more about handing it out and how useful that was for applying control. Eventually, and almost inevitably, he began to realise that money was a useful control method, along with drugs. Put the two together, and you could manage your own little empire. Of course, it wasn't that easy. He wasn't the only one who had worked out this obvious combination, and those who had were in many cases just as barking mad as he was, some far more so. But few of them were quite as clever as Glen, so he succeeded.

Zara was the nearest thing he had to a pet. From the moment he set eyes on her, he knew he could wrap her around his little finger and for some reason he never quite figured out himself, he decided he would. He had trapped a little cage bird. She came in useful as a sort of shield in certain social circles where he needed to mix occasionally. She was "nice" people liked her, and that gave him a sort of legitimacy. So did his children. He was quite proud of them in a way, and they gave Zara something to do. He liked owning things as well as controlling them. But this plague was driving him mad. He was losing control, and that could not happen. The half-baked scheme the government had come up with was insane. He really couldn't get his head around the fact that the millions he had earned and squirreled away over the years were gone and all that cash he had at home was useless if he couldn't prove that he had it legitimately.

Like everything else, the drugs trade was "just in time." You didn't keep warehouses full of the stuff. So, he had two problems: he could no longer resupply, and no one had any money to buy what he had. This latter problem he had a partial solution to, because one of his business fronts was a pawn shop. He was accepting gold and silver for payment and laundering it through the shop, where he had a smelter to melt the metals down into ingots and a reason to own them. It was this that caused the problem. The shop had electronic surveillance and security covering every inch of it. Fort Knox didn't come into it. At least, it had, until the plague hit. Now it was blind, deaf, and dumb.

He and his closest gang members had been running shifts trying to guard the place until he could work out what to do. It had a big safe, so they only had to guard it fully during the day. He had just arrived there with Darren, the nearest thing he had to a friend, when a rival gang turned up and a fight broke out. They fought them off, but Darren got shot. So here they were, at the doc's scruffy, looking semidetached house in a Liverpool suburb. Glen pulled into the Doc's crumbling, weed, filled drive. He didn't like being seen here, but he hadn't much choice, Darren wasn't up to walking round the corner. He helped him up to the door and banged on it hard.

A rather flustered, scruffy, and bleary, eyed Doc appeared, smelling of alcohol.

"What the hell?" he spluttered as Glen pushed past him into the dingy hallway.

"Darren's been shot. I need you to fix him up," said Glen. "Where should I put him?"

The Doc looked at both of them for a moment. "Bring him into the kitchen where I can see him better."

Glen helped Darren into the Doc's scruffy but surprisingly tidy kitchen and sat him down on a chair. The Doc took a quick look at the blood, soaked towel strapped in place with gaffer tape and said, "I can't help you. It's a bad stomach wound."

"Can't or won't?" Glen said, pulling a small automatic pistol from his trouser pocket.

"Look around you, Glen," said the Doc. "If you don't get him to a fully equipped operating theatre within the next hour, he'll be dead. Even if you do, his chances are fifty-fifty. He's got a bullet in his guts, there'll be internal damage and bleeding. He needs a blood transfusion. Do you really think I can help him?"

Glen said nothing. He gave the Doc a hard stare, and for a moment the Doc thought he might shoot him. Instead, Glen put the gun away and said, "Call an ambulance. Tell them Darren just turned up at the door. Darren, if you're asked, it was a drive, by shooting. You heard nothing, saw nothing, just felt the bullet hit you. OK?"

Darren nodded.

"Go with him, Doc. Darren will give you a number to ring so you can let me know how he gets on. I've got to get out of here." And he left.

The Doc called 999 and asked for an ambulance, telling them it was urgent, a gunshot wound. By the time the ambulance arrived, complete with an accompanying police car, Darren was unconscious.

While he waited, the Doc thought through what he should do. He knew he couldn't get involved in a gang war. The plague had caused major disruption in the drug business, and he was too tired and too angry with his own addictions to fight any longer. He told the police what had happened and gave them Glen's name. Normally, he would have been too afraid to do anything so stupid. But his animal instincts told him Glen was no longer a threat. Darren died on the way to the hospital, unaccompanied by the Doc, who had declined to go with him.

While all this happened, Glen had arrived back at his house. He'd decided he needed to get out, to do a runner. He would take what he had and go; the only question was where. He was wracking his brain and getting more and more frustrated as he drove through the estate gates and up to his house. He used his fob to open the garage door and, so wound up, failed to notice Zara's car was gone. He needed to get cleaned up and Zara needed to clean the car interior, fast. He burst into the kitchen and shouted for her as he headed to the bedroom to change. There was no response. He stopped and shouted again. Something clicked at the back of his mind, something was wrong. He ran back to the garage, and there it was: an empty space. Why the hell was the car gone? She wasn't using it; she had no need to. There was nowhere to go. He ran back upstairs, checked the bedrooms, and knew then, she had gone. It was too much. The suppressed rage took over. He screamed and howled, wrecking the house in a frenzy of destruction until he was exhausted.

If you'd asked Glen whether he thought he was lucky, he would have laughed and said something banal like, "You make your own luck." If he'd bothered to think about it, he would have assumed you needed to be clever, cleverer than the idiots around you. Luck had nothing to do with it. But his philosophy allowed for only a limited number of random events. He was about to find out that no one is immune to a combination of events over which they have no control. So far, his day had been bad enough. But what he didn't know was the disastrous effect his next-door neighbour would have on the rest of it, a person he had never met and never would. The house next door had been bought some months before, but he'd hardly seen anyone in it. With hindsight, he should have paid more attention.

The new owner was an ex-senior officer in the Lancashire Police Force. He'd retired years earlier and done well for himself working as a security consultant in Dubai. He'd bought the house as both a UK base and an investment. His children were grown and gone, and his wife was lying in the sun at their second house on the Costa de la Luz in Spain. He was supposed to be there with her, but thanks to the plague, he was stuck in the UK with nothing much to do. You didn't really need his years of police experience to know there was something not quite right about Glen. The car he drove was a bit of a giveaway.

So, partly out of boredom and partly because once a cop, always a cop, he'd been watching Glen closely. He'd made a few calls to old friends who had contacts and gathered that, while the police had no hard evidence, Glen was definitely "a person of interest." Or put another way, a considerable crook. He had a pretty good handle on the daily habits of the "crook's" wife and was even on nodding terms with her, as he often ate at the same café just up the road. He'd noticed the "crook" never went there and often wondered where he did eat. He had seen the car come and go, watched the wounded man helped in and out of the house, and observed the wife gather her children, pile them into the car, and drive off.

By this point, he had been on the phone to his local contacts, and a plan had formed. What Glen didn't know, while he was smashing the place up, was that two, armed policemen were already in position in his neighbour's back garden, ready to hop over the fence into his. They could hear the crashing, banging, and shouting, and were amazed to watch, through small gaps in the fence, as Glen took a sledgehammer to some of the ornamental pots in the garden, but they waited for the other backup to arrive. Glen had gone back into the house when the diversion they'd set up began. A police car had quietly driven up to the front of the house, coming through the big electronic gate, which the neighbour had opened for them. An ordinary, looking policeman got out, wearing what appeared to be a high, vis jacket. He walked up to the door and rang the bell.

The plan was simple, and that was what made it good. The house had the same layout as the neighbour's house and thanks to his careful observation, they were sure the patio doors at the back were open. When Glen answered the front door, the two at the back would hop over the fence and trap him. The officer at the door was wearing body armour, as was his colleague positioned to one side of the door. They were confident the security cameras were no longer working.

What happened to Glen next was quite simple: his luck ran out. He was still raging when the doorbell rang, and for some reason, this pushed him over the edge. He pulled the gun from his pocket, ready to shoot whoever had the nerve to ring his doorbell. He yanked the door open and was faced with a copper in a stupid yellow vest. He slammed the door shut again, spun around, and found himself facing two more cops, this time in full combat gear, pointing Heckler & Koch rifles at him. Unfortunately, in the act of spinning, he had raised the gun he was holding and was pointing it at them. They shot him, half a second apart, both rounds hitting him in the heart. He was dead before he finished collapsing to the ground. Both bullets went straight through him at that range, but fortunately for the young officer outside he didn't need the bullet proof vest, the door was a very expensive and bulletproof.

The UK was still technically under martial law, so the usual requirements regarding legal entry by armed police, search warrants, and so on didn't apply. Glen was a suspect in a shooting incident earlier that day, and the officers had heard and seen him commit acts of violence at the house. The subsequent search, which did take place with all the legal niceties in place, found large amounts of cash but no drugs. The drugs were found later, as more information came to light and other properties he owned were discovered and raided. No one had a clue where his wife and children were. The neighbour had given his ex-colleagues a full description of them and the car, but without TV and newspapers, they had only the radio to ask if anyone had seen them.

Zara

Fred liked to listen to the news on the radio in the kitchen and was on his own when the description of Zara, the kids, and their car came through, along with the story about a gangland crook who'd been shot dead in his home by the police. He was shocked at first, then dismayed, and finally relieved; it meant they were all safe. Sad, of course, that the little ones had lost their father, but in Fred's estimation, they were better off without him. He found Zara and Amy out in the garden, chatting about the flowers, and he was at a bit of a loss as to how to bring up the news he had to share. He stood there looking uncomfortable until Amy asked him what was wrong.

"I've just been listening to the local news on the radio. There's been a shooting, and they've put out a description of Zara, the kids, and the car," he said.

"A shooting?" said Zara.

"Yes," said Fred. "There's no easy way to tell you this. The police shot Glen this afternoon, sometime after you left."

Amy brought over a garden chair, and Zara sat down, putting her face in her hands. The tears didn't come then; it was too much to take in. She just looked tired and lost.

"Shot, you say?" she asked, looking at Fred.

"Er, yes. He's dead."

"Good grief," said Amy, getting a chair for herself.

"I'll give Neil a ring and let him know what's happened. He's a sensible lad, he can pop round, and we can give him all the details," said Fred, heading for the house.

"Who's Neil?" asked Zara.

"Our local community policeman," said Amy. "He's a nice lad. We're lucky to have him."

They sat in silence for a while until the children, who had been playing in the house, came out to disturb them. Zara wondered how she could possibly tell them they would never see Daddy again. Glen had never hurt them and at times had enjoyed playing with them, but he had always had a short attention span and could treat them with total indifference. She, on the other hand, spent a lot of time with them, and she guessed that as long as she was there, they would be okay.

"One thing's for sure," said Amy after a while. "You did the right thing today. You'll always know that. Imagine what might have happened if you'd still been there."

Zara just nodded.

The "nice lad" turned up after a while, and he fit the description, though Zara thought "lad" was a bit of a stretch. He made it plain that Zara had nothing to worry about, the police knew she had no part in what had happened. They were more concerned about her safety and that of the children. He was very pleased to find them all safe and sound. He talked to her about what had happened and why she had left when she did, and he arranged to come and collect her the following day so they could go to Liverpool for her to make a formal statement. For now, he would report back. Zara told him everything she could. After he left, she had something to eat, drank some more of Amy's nice Galician wine, and went to bed, where she slept a deep and dreamless sleep.

What followed was complicated and bittersweet. Neil was, at first, her liaison officer, then eventually her friend and advisor, before becoming her lover, husband, and finally business partner. All this time, she had to navigate the mess Glen had left behind.

The police were inclined at first to see her as an accomplice rather than a victim. What may have helped, in an odd way, was that she and Glen had never married, which placed her in a sort of ambivalent position to begin with. Over time, as the police began to dismantle his "business" empire, odd things popped up. Over the years they'd been together, Glen had occasionally insisted she sign documents for him. She never knew what they were, but it became apparent that, in law at least, she owned quite a property empire. Glen hadn't left a will, and the courts were intent on confiscating all his property as the proceeds of crime. Neil persuaded Zara, who really didn't want anything to do with any of it, to take on a solicitor he knew was clued up on the rules. The solicitor was happy to work on a "no win, no fee" basis, as long as he got 50% of the value of any assets he saved for Zara. She didn't like it; she wanted a clean break. But she had the children to think of, and she didn't want to rely on Fred and Amy forever. The legal arguments were going to take years to sort out. Her car was in her name, fairly new and very reliable. She had kept her scissors, combs, and brushes, and she was still a talented hairdresser. With Amy's contacts, she started a mobile hairdressing business. She was good at it, and her customers liked her.

Eventually, the solicitor began to make some headway, and capital started to come her way. She opened a salon. In time, she had a chain, bought a house of her own near Fred and Amy, and Neil eventually left his job with the police to help her manage the business. Fred and Amy led them on trips to northern Spain once the ferry service from Plymouth to Santander resumed. They tasted white Rioja and Verdejo, as well as her favourite Albariño, while travelling along the beautiful Costa Verde to Galicia. She never stopped thinking of Glen completely. That wasn't possible, even if she'd wanted to, because as her son grew up, he looked so much like his father. For a while, she worried about what he might turn into. She watched closely how he treated his friends, but he was a good kid who thought the world of his Uncle Fred and Aunt Amy. He did well at school; his teachers liked him, and he had a decent relationship with Neil. After they were married, Neil adopted him and his sister, and Glen's memory slowly faded into the past, only occasionally stabbing her in the heart without warning. But overall, she undoubtedly fell into that group of people for whom the plague had been of enormous benefit. She was a perfect example of the old platitude: It's an ill wind that blows no one any good.

Pay Day—Zero + 3 Months

The pressure to reestablish some form of economy had been enormous. Supply chains were becoming dangerously stretched, and food, drugs, essential chemicals, and even fuel were increasingly difficult to source. Huge efforts were made to maintain a basic supply system, but much of it depended on equipment. In many cases, normal computer controls could be bypassed to keep machinery running, but machines and production plants of any kind require maintenance. The usual network of suppliers and manufacturers that supported this effort had either closed or, where they could reopen, had limited resources. Everything was stretched to the limit. The steady state, the "status quo", was balanced on a knife edge. It was unsustainable in the long run, so enormous efforts were made to set up national banks and prepare for the day when everyone would receive some cash to spend.

First, the existing cash in the system had to be collected. Everyone had to open an account at their local branch of the National Bank and deposit any money they had. At the time, the UK government estimated about four billion notes of all denominations were in circulation. They weren't sure what percentage they would recover but expected around 90%, as the incentive to retain present value was high. Anyone with cash had to comply because all of it was going to be "re-designated." After Pay Day, any cash not "re-designated" would be worthless.

It was a massive undertaking. Each country planned to stamp and modify both notes and coins, sometimes even changing their denominations. This meant, for example, that if you had a £50 note, you had to deposit it; after Pay Day, it would (at least temporarily) become a £5 note. If you didn't register it, it would become worthless. In time, new notes and coins would be issued. Turning up with a suitcase full of £50 notes meant you needed a good explanation of how you'd obtained so much wealth; each bank branch had a resident police officer. Hoarding cash had become a criminal offence, so the police were having a field day raiding the homes of crime barons across the world in search of large stashes of cash and, as always, the lawyers were busy.

For most people, the value of their cash would be preserved in the national bank. If you had £100 in cash, after Pay Day, it would eventually buy you goods worth the equivalent of £1,000. Initially, though, you wouldn't be able to withdraw all of it. You could only spend the money you were given. In the UK, all paper money was re-designated as £5 notes or the equivalent of the old £50. Everything else stayed the same, but a £2 coin could now buy what a £20 note once did, a £1 coin £10, and the 50p coin the equivalent of £5. The 20p coin became the new £2, the 10p the pound, and the 5p the 50p coin. That worked fine until they reached the 1p coin, now worth 10 pence. The problem was how to get below 10p, so they cut many 1p coins in half, and for a while, the lowest denomination equated to 5p.

In the UK, this conveniently got rid of prices like "99p" but unfortunately fueled a degree of inflation. If you had foreign currency, the exchange rates were set at the rate at midnight the day before the plague hit, and by law, you had to deposit it at the bank, but you got a 100% swap with no fees. If you had gold, silver, or platinum above one Troy ounce in weight, you could have it valued and converted into money in your account. The government thereby built up its foreign currency and precious metal reserves.

All these instructions were passed on to the public via notice boards and radio, though only if you had an old analogue radio, as digital ones were useless. The BBC's television department was desperately trying to establish some sort of terrestrial transmission. Their main problem was the lack of receivers; almost all modern televisions used digital electronics and had some sort of internet connection, so they were useless. A couple of engineers thought it a shame to waste all those big screens, so they designed a simple receiver that could work with almost any type of screen. If you knew what you were doing, you could strip out the existing circuit boards and connect their box via an aerial to get a picture from a single channel.

They developed another box that let you use the screen via a laptop, which still existed in reasonable numbers. Many laptops had been turned off when the plague hit; if you could turn one on, it still functioned as a computer. Many had been donated to support vital services, but plenty remained in schools and private hands. The design and instructions for the boxes were published, and local engineers and enthusiasts began converting TVs. The government supported the effort by seizing stocks of electronic components, as the solution needed breadboards, discrete components, and the digital processing power of a laptop.

In some places, big screens were set up in village halls and canteens, and gradually, one or two houses on each street had them. It felt a bit like the 1950s all over again, with a very limited BBC output.

David and Caroline bumped into Dot and her family at their local bank branch one morning. Caroline had some Kruger Rands an aunt had given her. She had cashed them in at the local jewellers and was taking the credit note into the bank. David had a variety of foreign currencies to exchange, including a moderate sum in euros, so they set up a joint account that would see them through for a while. Dot and her family were lugging six glass demijohns that seemed to be full of one-pound coins.

"Me mum," explained Dot, "had them in a cupboard in the kitchen. She's been collecting them for years. This lot have been weighing demijohns and coins on my kitchen scales and reckon there's about £400 in each of them, so we're taking them to Bobby at the bank. He's an old friend and a coin collector, apparently, he's almost as excited as this lot. Me mum's given us all one each, and she wants the other two to pay for her funeral, or as she puts it, 'pay for mine more like it, I shouldn't wonder.'"

Caroline was horrified at this sentiment but couldn't help thinking Dot's mum had set her family up very well. Dot's two sons would have more than enough for a deposit on a house each, and Dot and her husband would be able to afford a very nice holiday eventually.

Dot asked how David's job application was going.

"OK, I think," said David. "I hadn't realised that working for the GPO would be a bit like working for a security firm. They do a lot of digging into your background as well as asking what you're qualified to fly."

"Are the planes safe?" asked Dot. Her husband gave her a rather withering look.

"Some are," said David. "Those that were parked up or in maintenance, as long as they had no power connected in any way, they weren't infected."

"I thought it was just the planes with a passenger internet connection that were a problem?" asked one of Dot's sons.

"Most planes also had satellite links with real, time monitoring of systems and engines, so they were infected even if they didn't have an internet link," said David. "The big problem is the lack of met and ground control. We can fly without GPS, but we need to avoid collisions, and we need to know what weather we're flying into. But they're working up systems that will allow some routes to open soon. Hopefully, I'll be flying one of them."

Dot looked at Caroline. "Are you OK with all this?" she asked.

"I can't say I'm thrilled," said Caroline, "but they seem to be making sure everything is in place. And David will be miserable if he can't fly. At the moment we want him to get the job, so I'll have mixed feelings if he gets it and mixed feelings if he doesn't. I can't win, Dot, so I've given up worrying about it."

"Very wise too," said Dot, patting Caroline's arm. The conversation moved on to how the potatoes were doing.

Some weeks later, they met up again on payday in the queue for the government cash handout. Everyone over the age of twenty-one was given £50, with another £10 for children under eighteen. Eighteen, to twenty-year-olds were given £20 each. From that day forward, the price of everything was divided by ten, regardless of what it was, from the price of a litre of petrol to an hour's consultation with a lawyer, to the price of a house. It was a criminal offence to try to avoid applying the reduction, and severe jail sentences were handed out to anyone found guilty. The government "wage" would be handed out weekly for two months, after which the situation would be reviewed.

There was a huge problem with mortgages. The decision to write off all debt was a great boon if you had a mortgage but was seen as grossly unfair to people paying rent, especially as landlords were going to be in the clover, with no mortgages to pay off. The government tried to be clever about this by proposing a tax on householders, which renters wouldn't have to pay, and which landlords were banned from passing on. This caused several riots, and by payday the problem was still unresolved.

Small businesses were largely left to their own devices to get going again, but large corporations were given lines of credit and backed by the National Bank. The long, term aim was to break up the National Bank and return to a system of competition, but the politics of that were tricky, to say the least. For now, the government wanted shops to open and businesses to start again in whatever way it could, though it was clear that it would be a slow process.

COBRA Post Payday

Prof. Davenport found himself summoned once again to a Cobra meeting, and once again an official car arrived to take him. He and his team had been pretty busy in the interim, and he wasn't particularly pleased about having to take time out for this. But he knew he had no choice, and he thought he might have some good news, of a sort.

The Prime Minister chaired the meeting again, and Davenport was a bit shocked at how much older and more tired she looked. She was a details person, not good at broad, brush politics, and the overwhelming specifics of this crisis would have been enough to exhaust anyone. He was pleased to see the reassuring presence of Lady Arbuthnot, whose calm, practical, no, nonsense approach was always a boost to morale.

"OK, ladies and gentlemen, thank you for attending today," said the PM. "We have a full agenda to get through, but I'd like Lady Arbuthnot to start by reviewing where we are with food supplies."

"Well, Prime Minister, at the moment we are still feeding most of the nation via the feeding stations we set up. The main difference is that we're now charging for the meals. I'm not sure this is a good idea, but the Treasury insisted.

Some small shops have opened, selling groceries and bread to those who prefer to eat at home. We've made some progress in teaching the general public basic cooking skills, but we're not convinced we could move to formal rationing if we had to."

"Rationing?" asked the PM. "Is that still a possibility?"

"It may have to be," said Lady Arbuthnot. "The way we've been feeding the nation so far is a form of rationing. We need to buy a significant amount of food from Europe, and I'm told the reserves we have to pay for it aren't endless.

It's a moot point at the moment, though, the main problem is still shipping enough in. The Channel Tunnel has been a lifesaver, and the ferry companies have done a great job getting their ships working again. We're getting some supplies through 'roll-on, roll-off' container shipments, and a few from the smaller automated container docks, but it's all barely enough.

We've been in long and detailed negotiations with some of the big fast, food outlets to see if we can issue ration cards."

"What, for a Quarter Pounder?" piped up one of the civil servants, laughing. Lady Arbuthnot gave him a withering look.

"More probably chicken McNuggets and fries," she said, somehow managing to make the statement drip with sarcasm. "I doubt we'll be able to supply them with enough beef for a Big Mac."

"But you're proposing to issue ration cards for fast food meals?" asked the PM.

"I'm afraid so, Prime Minister. I know it sounds hard to swallow, if you'll forgive the pun, but these companies have well established supply chains. They're everywhere, and they're popular. If we use them, it might prove an efficient way of distributing food.

The only problem is agreeing on what people will be able to get for their coupons. As you know, Prime Minister, the UK can't feed itself without imports. As I mentioned earlier, our ability to access everything we need is still limited, and even if that improves, we now need to pay for imports out of our cash reserves."

"Yes," said the PM. "Of course we need something to trade with, to earn the money to buy the food." She turned to one of the grey suits whom Prof. Davenport hadn't seen before.

"Doctor Brook," she said. "How is the assessment of our manufacturing capacity progressing?"

Davenport thought the man looked tired and sad.

"It's pretty depressing, Prime Minister. As you know, successive governments over the last decades pushed for improvements in productivity across the economy. One of the few sectors to respond reasonably well was manufacturing, they had to, in order to survive.

In the modern age, that means a heavy reliance on computerisation. Vehicle manufacture is dead in the water; it'll take years to get going again at any useful volume. It isn't just the robots; the whole supply chain is gone, together with the design base. They don't actually have any drawings anymore, and no means to reproduce them even if they could.

Logistics are a mess. We have huge warehouses stacked to the gills with stuff, all of it listed on computer inventories that no longer exist. Since everything was identified by barcodes, we haven't a clue what's stored on miles and miles of shelves, and even less idea who owns it, if anyone does now that so many companies have gone bust."

He paused and looked at the Prime Minister, whose head was down. He took a deep breath and carried on.

"It's little comfort, Prime Minister, but the rest of the world is in the same boat. The problems we face aren't unique to the UK. We may have restored the ability for people to buy and sell goods again, but the systems we had in place to manufacture and supply those goods are in pieces.

We're just about keeping the lights on and supplying clean water for now, and we've managed to keep some trains and buses running, but if we don't resurrect some parts of our manufacturing base soon, even these small successes will be in danger. They all need spares for maintenance.

As for producing anything we can sell abroad to pay for our food, that could take years."

"That seems a rather pessimistic view. Why years?" asked the Prime Minister.

"Because all the machines we used to manufacture goods had electronic control systems of some sort, most of them digital. It will take a huge effort to get them working again, assuming we could access the electronics to repair them. But we can't. Apart from the components we may have in stock in warehouses, and without proper inventories, we can't access new supplies. There simply aren't any to be had at the moment."

"Ah," said Prof. Davenport. "I might have a suggestion about that."

Everyone looked at him.

"Suggest away," said the PM.

The Professor swallowed and plunged in.

"As you know, the advice I gave to the UN conference was that all damaged electronic goods should be thought of as 'poisoned' by the plague and destroyed." He paused but was met by silence. "We think that may have been a bit hasty. We've been devising ways to rescue some microprocessor components. There isn't much we can do with ASICs, but we think we can reformat and reuse FPGAs."

"I have no idea what you were talking about at the end there," said the PM. "But how does any of this help our trade balance?"

"We may be able to do two things. First, we could provide the electronics industry with a large percentage of what it needs to get these systems working again. And we'd be able to trade in electronic components," said the Professor. "We've been working on equipment and processing protocols that mean we can safely handle old, printed circuit boards. We don't need to scrap all the damaged computers, as we first suggested. Instead, we can strip them down and start selling usable electronic components. If we scale up the process, we could sell millions.

"It's a novel process we can protect with patents, though no doubt others will eventually copy it. In the long run, the old electronics manufacturers will get started again. But at present, they're struggling to get back online. The consensus is that we should develop a new code that will be plague-resistant before manufacturing new processor chips. Meanwhile, everyone wants to patch up existing equipment and control systems, so these clean components would be like gold dust."

This was met with silence for a few moments.

"So, let me see if I've understood this properly," said the PM. "You're proposing that we mobilise a whole new industry in the UK, rescuing and selling electronic components?"

"That's correct," said the Professor. "The kit we've devised is relatively easy to reproduce, and we can train people to use it very quickly. We'd need to set up production lines to strip down the hardware safely and remove the components we need, and other lines to reformat them. We have a technique that guarantees the end-product is plague-free, and we believe we can set up good quality assurance systems so nothing dangerous gets through."

"But presumably this would be a temporary effort," said the Prime Minister. "Eventually, you'd simply run out of computers to strip down."

"That's true," replied the Professor. "But if we move quickly and establish ourselves as the leader in this technology, we can start importing dead computers from all over the world. We know the electronics component industry will get going again eventually, but demand will be enormous for some time to come. We may very well be able to undercut new component prices even when production ramps up. Besides, we'll be able to get new computer manufacturing up and running before anyone else, so we'll be able to sell both components and finished products."

"Would this help us, Dr. Brook?" the Prime Minister asked, turning to the grey man, who was looking hard at Prof. Davenport.

"In time, yes." He paused for a few moments and continued. "We'd have to prioritise which parts of the supply chain need the most urgent help first, and we'd have to coordinate and mobilise all our electronics design and manufacturing capability. But over time, it would certainly secure what we have and start to get things moving."

"What do you need?" asked the PM. "No, never mind, you'll get what you need. Talk to Derek, the business secretary, and let me know what the plan is. And thank you, that's the first bit of positive news I've had in a while."

The Aftermath

For years, the push had been towards "globalisation," which really meant exporting low-skilled jobs. Manufacturing had always been seen in the UK as awkward, difficult, and messy, a sort of clumsy pastime for tradesmen, at least in the eyes of the Oxbridge arts graduates who ran the country. Sitting at a desk using a computer to make money was obviously a more civilised thing to do, so why not export all the messy stuff abroad where it could be done so much cheaper?

The companies that survived this attitude in the UK, and, to some extent, most of Western Europe and America, were modern, high-tech outfits with high productivity. In other words, they relied heavily on IT, robots, and highly automated equipment with very few staff. The machines cost the same wherever you bought them, so provided you could keep your overheads down, you could compete.

Globalisation had arrived because of a complex mix of events, but high among these in importance were containerisation, the development of supply chain management, and, of course, computers and the internet. The manufacturing techniques developed by the Japanese had become ubiquitous, and of these, "Just in Time" was pretty much universally accepted.

The days when large companies were run by "Captains of Industry" were long gone. Boards of directors made up of representatives from the different elements of business had been replaced by boards mainly involved in financial management. You had to have an MBA to climb the ladder in industry in the modern era, which meant you had been taught that you increased a company's profits by cutting costs. Storing spare parts cost money and meant capital lying idle, so buffer stocks were abandoned in favour of the items you needed arriving as you needed them, "Just in Time." Car manufacturers might very well find the tyres they were unloading from a supplier were still warm, having left the final autoclave just a few hours earlier.

This approach had become ubiquitous, so engineering spare parts did not exist in large quantities. Most large-scale manufacturers in the global era ran assembly plants rather than manufacturing plants. They bought in all the individual components from a long supply chain of subcontractors, and many of these were based in third-world countries where labour was cheap. But these supply chains were complex beasts and relied enormously on computer science and software in one form or another.

The products were designed using computers, and the designs were stored in digital form. The subcontractors had to be able to use CAD to survive. The plague destroyed all of this. This group of leading-edge, successful companies were all dead in the water. Car production, which relied so heavily on computer design and robotics, would take years to recover.

Large-scale food processing was defunct, along with much of the food supply chain, because many of the big agricultural companies used high-tech kit to bring in the crops and process them. What manufacturing base the UK had left was heavily computerised and had been largely wiped out, literally wiped out, because the big manufacturers not only lost the means to assemble their products, they also lost their design databases. Even if they could replace the computers, they would have to start from scratch.

The situation was far worse than at the end of WWII. The war had caused massive damage across the world, and during the war period, investment in infrastructure in the UK had stopped in favour of supplying the war effort. At the end of the war, the UK was bankrupt, and its railways, public transport, and industrial base were largely worn out, but they still existed.

After the plague, the UK was as bankrupt as any other country, but it had hardly any functioning industrial base, and its agricultural sector wasn't big enough to feed the nation. Winter was approaching, and the country was pretty much entirely dependent on imported energy. Without the demands of industry, the requirement would be significantly reduced, but now that countries could start to trade again, the UK had to ask: "With what?"

At first, the politicians were very pleased with themselves, believing they had managed to rescue the capitalist system. Money could circulate again, people could buy and sell goods, and trade could happen. But it soon began to dawn on everyone that the kind of trade they had once known no longer existed. There was an increasing need to mobilise as much effort as possible to service the core requirements of food, water, power, and public transport.

Politicians are obsessed with politics, and some are good at it. Civil servants are also obsessed with politics, but for them, the obsession is with the internal politics of the civil service. Their understanding of how things worked outside of government was limited. How corporate companies operated, and the finer points of manufacturing and supply chains, remained a mystery to them, far beyond their personal experience or understanding, so when it became obvious that Payday was only a partial solution, and the world remained in an awful mess, they were at a loss about what to do next.

The total disappearance of the City of London as a financial centre took some time to sink in. The big insurance houses were gone. People who had insisted on holding physical share certificates rather than online versions could still claim ownership, but generally, they held shares in companies that were now largely worthless. The banks and hedge funds had all collapsed, and the politicians no longer had nice, lucrative retirement jobs waiting for them.

Utilities still had value, but they also faced myriad problems. Some poorer countries were perversely better off: they still had significant artisan workforces and had inherited much of the West's redundant machine tools. India and Pakistan managed to restart the bones of a textile industry, but it was only a shadow of its former self, barely capable of meeting domestic demand. Exports, while potentially valuable to the national coffers, were still some way off.

The UK was in trouble. It had reverted to the 1950s but was now bereft of the manufacturing capacity it once had. It couldn't feed itself and couldn't afford to buy what it needed without bartering goods or services. It would be decades before governments could run huge deficits again and finance them through borrowing. The nation had cast itself off from the European Union and, unlike the 1950s, could expect little help from America.

Across the country, every lathe, milling machine, and any manufacturing kit that didn't require a computer to drive it was brought back into service. Anyone who still had the skills to use them was called upon. Retired teachers from further education establishments found newfound status in society. Great effort was put into jury-rigging production lines for vital items like drugs, finding ways to make them without computer controls. In some cases, portions of the great mass of unemployed were recruited to sit at benches all day, stamping out pills by hand.

Globalisation rapidly went into reverse. Along with it went high productivity, and millions found themselves out of work. There seemed to be an obvious need to get everyone into manufacturing replacement electronics, but that required a supply chain. And of all the industries that existed, the electronics component sector was perhaps the most reliant on computer-controlled manufacturing. These systems had to be repaired before any new products could be made.

Work began on reclaiming as many electronic components as possible. The armed forces helped with logistics, partly because they had nothing else to do and partly because they were keen to see if they could replace their ruined kit, though it was a forlorn hope. Useless computers and servers were collected from across the country and brought to processing plants that were hastily set up. These operations needed people power above all else, and recruits were rapidly trained to remove, recycle, test, catalogue, and store millions of electronic components, both discrete parts and processor chips.

Across the country, electronics engineers began designing and building circuits to replace the machine control systems. A multitude of Heath Robinson concoctions appeared, made up of proper PCBs and bits of breadboard. But eventually, even the five-axis CNC lathes began working again.

Old drawing boards were dragged out from dusty corners and reconditioned, and retired engineers started training a new generation of draughtsmen in the use of pencil and paper. Working computers that still existed became like gold dust. Slowly, the ability to make and repair grew. The UK developed a lucrative export market for electronic components, enough, at least, to pay for some food imports and energy supplies.

Cottage industries started to appear, with enterprising people manufacturing writing paper, pens, and ink. Small shops made a comeback, especially local bakeries. Charity shops rapidly had to change format as second-hand goods developed real value. These items could now be sold rather than given away, especially clothing, so the shops had to start paying for stock rather than relying on donations.

Dressmaking and tailoring saw something of a resurgence, as did the World War II idea of make do and mend. Spare parts for cars were available at first, but soon became rare and very expensive, returning to old pre-Payday prices. Gradually, tyres and batteries began to reappear as companies jury-rigged more production lines, but in much smaller quantities and at much higher costs. This might have led to rampant inflation, but people simply did without. If you couldn't afford to fix your car, you used public transport, people had grown used to it and you sold your car for a good price for spares. The roads, having become busy for a while, gradually emptied again.

Unemployment was massive, far above Depression era levels and remained high for a long time, until gradually, and very slowly, the economy began to grow again.

People had simply taken the algorithm for granted. The fact that it had crept into almost every corner and crevice of the human experience never occurred to the great unwashed, or, for that matter, the great and the good. People had, of course, expressed concern about the influence of social media, mainly because of the way it affected the general media and threatened some commentators' precious positions. But even here, it wasn't seen as the advancement of yet another algorithm. Mankind's increasing dependence was ignored.

The influence of the algorithm had therefore grown silently and remorselessly. Dependency on something that was never designed for the purpose had become absolute, while politicians played at "weaponising" software. In the modern world, without the algorithm, cloth could neither be spun nor woven, cars could not be built, the distribution of goods could not operate, satellites and rockets could not be built or launched, and the lack of GPS for shipping and even large, scale agriculture caused havoc. Sailors could learn to navigate by dead reckoning and the stars again, but there wasn't much point if the computer used to control your ship's engines was defunct. Stripping out the sensor system and hot-wiring a massive marine engine was not for the faint-hearted. Even if it worked, could you manage without radar?

Modern ships are too big to set sail without the ability to see where they are going in all conditions. Trade had evaporated. It was difficult to fill a mega, size container ship and impossible to unload it at a largely robotic port handling system. And so it went on: from home entertainment to supermarkets no longer running on bar codes, everything had to be reorganised to work.

When the concept of the algorithm had first emerged, back in the days when computers occupied rooms and were programmed using punched tapes, the fact that algorithms were rather delicate entities, easily disrupted, didn't matter. Once you had them working properly, there was nothing to interfere with them, and no thought was given to the fact that they might continue working for decades. The internet, among other developments, changed all that and exposed algorithms to all sorts of dangers. A whole new industry, the IT security sector, had grown up just to defend algorithms, and it had been busy. It had a lot to defend. With hindsight, it would perhaps be reasonable to ask if the system that had developed was sustainable. Maybe what was needed was something else.

David did eventually get a job flying for the GPO. Planes were available, and others could be scavenged for spares if need be. In fact, a small rump of what had been Rolls-Royce Aero Engines set itself up to manage the scavenging and maintenance process. The company no longer had any computerised databases, but it did have experienced technicians and some written maintenance manuals. There was even a plan, eventually, to try and start building VC10s again, as the plane still had its enthusiasts and there was enough of its design on paper to allow manufacture. It depended on the ability of Rolls-Royce to build new engines using old manufacturing techniques, which was a separate question.

Some basic ground control had been established at the airports, along with "meteorology by phone" and a network of radio beacons. But there was no such thing as automatic landing; you had to land it yourself. It was estimated that they could continue flying mail and some freight for at least ten years this way. After that, no one was too sure.

But David had a job. Caroline was expecting and keeping herself very busy being a housewife. It wasn't the career she had dreamt of, but she knew the two of them were pretty lucky really. Once the baby arrived, she would not have a lot of time to think about it. In truth, if she was honest with herself, the career she had flogged away at had been a lousy waste of time anyway, and she really didn't miss it.

David never made it back to Helsinki, but he did fly to Stockholm. Using his employee discount, he paid for quite a large, heavy crate to be flown out. It was collected by Agneta's uncle, who was still working up there. It contained the bike and all the other stuff she had lent him, with a thank, you gift and a heartfelt letter from Caroline. Agneta was thrilled to bits. Life was beginning to get tough. She had a new boyfriend, and he would find most of the contents of the crate pretty cool, even the bike. It was always useful to have something to sell or barter. Overweening sentimentality, which had become such a powerful feature of the "Snowflake" generation's society, was rapidly melting away like pink candy floss in the rain.

The world had lost technology before. Many sophisticated societies with clever technology had come and gone, though in the past the technology was generally limited to civil engineering. The Romans had plumbing and sewage, handling skills that were lost for almost 2,000 years. Truth be told, how they made cement is still a bit of a mystery. But ancient civilisations and empires had not been quite so totally global in their reach. Never before had the whole world had such a dependency on a single form of technology that was wiped out so quickly.

It was a monumental disaster, and lots and lots of people died because of it, either directly in crashing aircraft, or indirectly, like those who could not access the drugs they needed because the factories could not function without their computer systems, or those who died of famine because the poor governments they had simply collapsed. The very poor suffered through abandonment by organisations that could no longer support them, and in many places, societies collapsed into anarchy with the usual results.

Plenty of idiots had guns and ammunition, though the major terrorist groups suddenly found themselves isolated with no money and no communications. It didn't stop them being idiots, and they still went around intimidating, murdering, and raping the weak and innocent, but in isolated spots where people often fought back. It was a mess, but a mess with a chance.

Many of the more visionary people wondered if it could not be used as an opportunity to put right previous mistakes, to take the opportunity to reform as the world was rebuilt. A movement did emerge to fight the idea of "economic growth" and "the consumer society," and to try to control the worst side effects of an absolute desire to maximise profit margins under all circumstances.

Ideas that had been suggested in the past about measuring well, being rather than wealth, and a wish to avoid going back to "gross domestic product," gained some traction in the teeth of opposition from a large, reactionary old guard. Crackpot religious sects popped up all over the place, using the opportunity to gain control over the weak and confused. Utopia it wasn't, but a feeling that things had to change permeated the people of the world, and so, gradually, it did…

Humankind has caused and experienced many massive disasters in its relatively short history and has so far, survived. But this was an odd one, because it affected so many people across the planet in such a short time, and in the same way. Disparate governments with wildly different political ideologies were generally forced to act quickly in broadly the same way and equally forced to act in reasonably close unison to get the world economy started again.

The better-run democracies moved quickly to secure the basics for their populations. In the short term, while everyone lost all the money they had, everyone was in the same boat. Many still had their homes and food to eat. They could use public transport for free and had all their utilities for free. Many carried on working if they could. The health services took on volunteers to try and sort out the mess they were in, with a lack of records and a mass of now useless equipment.

Crime didn't disappear, but it reduced for a while. A sort of black market started to emerge, with cigarettes, drugs, and alcohol as a form of currency. But you could only trade them for each other or to pay for sex and even this diminished after Payday. For quite a while, nothing had any real value. Everything was reduced to basics.

An odd side effect of this was that, after the initial shock, people settled down to find they were suddenly under a lot less pressure. They didn't need to strive anymore. There was a blessed release from the pressure of social media. People started to talk to one another and help each other. The roads were quiet, kids could play on the streets, and millions of bikes that had been gathering dust in garages and sheds were cleaned up and put back into service. Strangely, for many people in the world, life improved rather than deteriorated.

But these were mainly people living in democracies with the rule of law. Payday was supposed to be a universal event. But in the countries that were blatant kleptocracies, the outcome was always going to be bad for the poor. Most had been taken over in military coups, but that just replaced one type of corrupt dictator with another, all of whom were clearly of the opinion that dividing the value of everything by ten was a good idea for everyone else, but not for them. So the poor of the world remained poor. A few of the nastier dictators got their just deserts, but generally the replacements were little better and set about stealing what they could.

India's Payday had been very complex. Close to a third of the population lived below the poverty line. Giving them all a hundred rupees would simply have meant that the local thugs and loan sharks became very rich. This whole section of Indian society was cash, based anyway, with few, if any, bank accounts, despite efforts in the past to change this. Dividing the price of the basic staples would help, but not if what they earned was also divided by ten, because they earned so little to start with. India had its own version of what the rest of the world did. It gave money to roughly two, thirds of its population, those who had been paid a salary from the lower end to the upper middle class. The government set a pre-event earnings level. If you could demonstrate that you had been at that level or above it (up to a certain limit), you were given cash. At the same time, it put a huge effort into establishing and enforcing a sensible minimum wage so that the poor didn't starve.

It worked, after a fashion. Soon, while India's poor were back to their normal desperate state, it was perhaps slightly less desperate than it had been.

America was under martial law for quite a time, with the National Guard patrolling the streets. They soon became twitchy about the fact that a lot of the citizens they were supposed to be protecting had better guns than they did. It had finally sunk in that it really wasn't a good idea to let the general public own military assault weapons. Huge, angry protests ensued when they started confiscating them in some states. It was the first true crack in the dam of America's addiction to guns.

There was, however, little doubt that the world was a mess. Globalisation and interconnectivity had somehow made a significant contribution to the world's levels of overpopulation. An incredible amount of the underlying algorithmic infrastructure that had been underpinning all this had been destroyed. Medicine had been thrown back at least fifty years, no MRI scans, no robotic keyhole surgery. Modern laboratory testing and DNA analysis disappeared overnight, as did most medical records.

It would take an age to get the internet up and running again, and people wanted something different this time. They wanted the return of the convenience of mobile phones, but, having tasted freedom from the tyranny of social media, they wanted something less all, consuming and invasive. They wanted something safer, that wasn't controlled by American mega, companies that seemed too large to police.

Travel and trade needed, more than anything, the meteorological system reinstalling, as well as GPS. But this latter boon really meant getting back into space, something that was pretty much impossible without computers to help. Valiant efforts based on using hydrogen balloons and drones couldn't really replace satellites. The Met Office had to re-establish its post, war systems, and the Brits went back to moaning about how useless the weather forecast was.

So the Earth turned. Humankind survived. Consumption, for a while, collapsed, so CO_2 emissions dropped and the atmosphere recovered by a useful amount. People tried very hard to learn from past mistakes, which was noble but futile, as they all carried on making new ones.

It took some time for the pundits, politicians, philosophers, and economists of the world to fully understand just what a massive effect the plague had had. The initial natural reaction was to try to get back to what had been "normal" to get the world economy working again. To a limited extent, this succeeded. But it soon became apparent that the old economy was gone. A world in which massive amounts of money flowed around electronically no longer existed, and it wasn't going to exist for the foreseeable future. Trade had to be in goods, not data or information, and you either paid by cheque or cash.

Epilogue

Obviously, this is a work of complete fiction. The possibility that all they algorithms on the planet are wiped out at once is vanishingly small. But partial collapses, are already happening. There is an ever-increasing gap in understanding between the technology we all rely on and the people who manage it. As I write this the people responsible for air safety in the US still use floppy discs when lots of young people don't know what they are.

Society has never lived through a period where technology has developed and advanced at such a rate and our systems of government and leadership have not advanced by any noticeable amount. It is not a good position to find ourselves in. Don't give up on cash just yet.

If you enjoyed reading this book in all its eccentric, British, quirkiness, please leave a review on the platform where you bought it. Thank you!

AMAZON.CO.UK.

Thanks

Dean / Risby

Printed in Dunstable, United Kingdom